What people are saying about Jenny Gardiner's books:

"A fun, sassy read! A cross between Erma Bombeck and Candace Bushnell, reading Jenny Gardiner is like sinking your teeth into a chocolate cupcake...you just want more."

--Meg Cabot, NY Times bestselling author of Princess Diaries, Queen of Babble and more, on Sleeping with Ward Cleaver

"With a strong yet delightfully vulnerable voice, food critic Abbie Jennings embarks on a soulful journey where her love for banana cream pie and disdain for ill-fitting Spanx clash in hilarious and heartbreaking ways. As her body balloons and her personal life crumbles, Abbie must face the pain and secret fears she's held inside for far too long. I cheered for her the entire way."

--Beth Hoffman, NY Times bestselling author of *Saving CeeCee Honeycutt* on *Slim to None*

"Jenny Gardiner has done it again--this fun, fast-paced book is a great summer read."

--Sarah Pekkanen, NY Times bestselling author of *The Opposite of Me*, on *Slim to None*

"As Sweet as a song and sharp as a beak, *Bite Me* really soars as a memoir about family--children and husbands, feathers and fur--and our capacity to keep loving though life may occasionally bite."

--Wade Rouse, bestselling author of At Least in the City Someone Would Hear Me Scream

Blue Collar Romeo

(book four of the Royal Romeos series)
by Jenny Gardiner

Copyright © 2017 by Jenny Gardiner
Cover art by Kim Killion, The Killion Group, Inc.

ISBN: 978-1944763039

Chapter One

GISELE Hornsby kept pinching herself, even as she brushed on a third application of mascara, hoping a bit more makeup might distract from her bloodshot, hungover eyes. She still couldn't believe she was here, in Monaforte, a guest at a romantic Christmastime royal wedding, headed to her first "royal engagement" as her brother Parker's plus-one for *the* event of the season. It was enough to make even the most hungover of girls swoon.

She'd arrived in the fairy-tale country of Monaforte, a small European principality nestled between Italy and Switzerland, with her brother—a college friend of the groom, Prince Luca—in time to attend the many scheduled prenuptial events. They even got to stay as royal guests in an apartment in the palace —where all the royal people lived! Life could not get any cooler.

Gisele had spent her first full day in the country touring Porto Castello, the charming and historic capital of Monaforte, with her new friend Valentina Romeo, a royal cousin of Luca's, and for some undisclosed reason, her brother's adversary. Gisele was determined to get to the bottom of the mystery: Why had Valentina thrown daggers at Parker whenever he looked her way? And why had her normally chill brother suddenly turned surly.

She mistakenly thought tequila would unlock the answer, and proceeded to get both Valentina and herself sloppy drunk in the middle of the afternoon at a quaint little seaside pub, though she never did get to the root of the problem before Valentina's superhot brother Tomasso stopped them from making complete fools of themselves in public.

He was at an advantage, what with his jaw-dropping good looks: tall with wavy, dark hair, the most expressive amber eyes, broad shoulders and chest, and a truly perfect tight butt tucked into a sexy pair of jeans. What self-respecting girl who hadn't been laid in a long while wouldn't capitulate to the guy? So although the two women were having far too much fun for a weekday afternoon, they relented, paid the bar bill, and returned to the palace at his insistence, where Gisele promptly passed out for a few hours before the evening's royal bash was to start.

Her alarm went off with just enough time to get ready for the party, to be held at the country home of Luca's brother and heir apparent to the throne, Prince Adrian and his wife Emma. As soon as the phone blared its reveille, she made a mental note to switch her alarm from the preprogrammed "marimba" tone to something with a little less sensory overload for her throbbing brain next time. Though there wouldn't be a next time—she'd also made a mental note to remember that tequila only led to pain and suffering after the fun wore off. For that very reason, she popped a couple of Advil to tamp down the headache that threatened to ruin her evening, slapped on some face paint, and hoped no one would be the wiser to her flagging state of mind.

After slinking into an above-the-knee, black, tiered tulle

cocktail dress with spaghetti straps and a sexy open back, she twisted her long, blond waves into a loose side-braid, then slid on a pair of black Stuart Weitzman strappy sandals with heels that showed off her runner's legs perfectly. She turned to her side in front of the mirror, smoothing down her gown at the waistline, then applied a coat of dark pink lipstick, fluttered her lashes over her bright blue eyes, pressed her lips together, and nodded to herself.

"Perfect," she said. "No one will be the wiser that I feel like complete crap."

She grabbed her jacket from the closet and stepped into the living room to join Parker, who stood by the door, coat already on and buttoned up, arms crossed, eyes fixed on his watch, and tapping his toe impatiently.

"What?" Gisele said, grinning. "I'm like thirty seconds late."

Parker threw her the side-eye. "Thirty seconds give or take five minutes. Besides, if you hadn't been preoccupied with invoking my good name in conversation with your equally drunk friend this afternoon, just think—you could have actually been early. Now we'll probably not even get a seat on the bus." The palace was providing transportation for all of the guests to Luca's country estate.

Gisele rolled her eyes. "I love you, Parks, but you can be a little fastidious sometimes. Relax, sweet brother," she said. "It's all good. There will definitely be a seat on the bus. Plus, I didn't make anything worse for you and I got to meet Valentina's cute brother. I'd say it's a win-win."

He shook his head. "You were never good at keeping score, G." He reached for her hand and pulled her out the door. "Sticking your nose into my business means I lose. Now, come on, or I'm going to get stuck sitting on that

Valentina woman's lap and at this rate, Lord knows what sort of torture she'd impose on me for that transgression."

Parker didn't exactly have to sit on Valentina's lap but did have to tuck into the next row up from her, the only seats left on the bus thanks to Gisele's timing. After a little shuffling at the behest of the girls, Gisele wedged in next to Valentina, which meant Parker ended up sitting next to Tomasso. Gisele threw a hard glare at her brother.

"What?" he said, squinting his eyes at her.

She knit her brows and nudged her head in the direction of his seatmate, trying to convey that she wanted to sit next to Tomasso. But her dense brother simply frowned, his lips pursed to send her a silent message to leave him the hell alone.

Grrrr. Can't a girl get a little one-on-one time in a dark bus with a gorgeous Italian man? She'd have to work on that one a bit.

Gisele's eyes opened wide in amazement as the bus approached the estate, which was surrounded by a tall brick wall and draped with holly and pine roping entwined with white lights for the holiday season. The bus passed a large, brick guardhouse flanked by stone-faced men with bright red uniforms and tall furry hats—what was with royals and those hats?—then continued along a tree-lined driveway for a mile or so before finally stopping in the pebbled parking area of the palatial Georgian country estate.

As they lined up to leave the bus, Gisele couldn't help but lean gently against Tomasso. After all, people were clamoring to get out; there was no room to move. That was her excuse, anyhow, and she enjoyed feeling his solid body pressed to hers in the dark, even if she did have a heavy coat as a niggling barricade. At least it let her fantasize for a minute about what being body-to-body horizontally with the man, rather than vertically, would be like as she waited to step down from the damned bus.

They followed one another up the slate walkway, entering through massive oversized doors hung with giant Christmas wreaths. As two butlers greeted guests and collected coats, she tried to stick close to Parker so she wouldn't feel too out of place, but no sooner did he hand off his coat than he disappeared, no doubt fleeing Valentina's presence and leaving Gisele to stand by the doorway. Not knowing a soul, she felt like a complete idiot standing there like a girl lost in the woods in a fairy tale. She even pretended to wave to a couple of strangers who responded by looking at her as if she was daft.

"I'd offer you a drink, but that's probably the last thing you want right about now," she heard a deep voice from behind say.

She turned to see Tomasso, stylish in a dark blue Ermenegildo Zegna suit she recognized as similar to one her brother had tried on when they'd gone shopping for the wedding back home in New York. Gisele had persuaded Parker to spend big bucks to be well clothed for this week of festivities. Staring a beat too long at Tomasso only reminded her how much she loved a man in a well-fitted, sexy Italian suit.

She rolled her eyes. "I'm not sure if I should reprimand

you for spoiling our good fun or thank you for it." She rubbed her temples against the throb of the headache that even ibuprofen didn't seem to touch. "But, I think my only choice tonight is to double down against that evil tequila. Maybe temper it with some more genteel champagne?"

Tomasso reached for two glasses of champagne from a passing waiter and handed her a flute.

"In that case, here's to the hair of a somewhat softer dog," he said, clinking glasses with her.

"Ugh. I prefer my canines to be of the four-legged variety, thanks," she said. "Not the kind that somehow mysteriously penetrate your brain and bark and scratch to get out while you feel as if your eyeballs are going to pop right out of their sockets."

"You make drinking shots sound so pleasant."

"Shots are never pleasant after the fact. They only seem like a great idea while you're in the middle of doing them."

"You could say the same thing about relationships," he said with a grimace.

She lifted an eyebrow. "Well, if that's not the most cynical comment du jour, especially considering you're here for a romantic wedding."

He rolled his eyes. "You don't buy into that happily ever after nonsense, do you?" he said. "These things are little more than mergers. Sort of like two businesses that think they can work together, but when it comes down to it, one of the two ends up suffering for it."

Gisele shook her hand as if she'd touched something hot. "Wow," she said. "I'm surprised you even bothered to show for this. Why on earth are you celebrating something you clearly don't see worthy of any such joy?"

He crossed his arms and scratched his chin as if lost in

contemplation over her question. "Let's see... Because my mother made me?" he said. "Besides, it's more like a family reunion, and who doesn't like a family reunion?"

Gisele pursed her lips. She and Parker had never had the chance to indulge in things like family get-togethers, what with their very broken family.

"I wouldn't know," she said, throwing back a gulp of champagne.

"Thirsty?" he said, cocking his eyebrow and grinning.

"I'd rather tamp down my hangover with good champagne than draw attention to the fact that I don't exactly have a family with whom I can commune."

"Homeless, are you?"

"More like orphaned."

"I'm sorry." He scrunched his nose. "I was only joking. Didn't mean to poke fun at you."

"Poke away," she said. "Families come in all shapes and sizes. Mine happens to be minuscule and made up of me and my brother Parker."

"Funny, Parker practically seems like family to us," he said. "After spending so many holidays with him I feel like he's my brother from another mother."

She shrugged. "Great for Parker. Now he's got an extended family. Where does that leave me?"

"I'm sure we can throw you in as an honorary family member. You'll be the twofer."

"Gee, that's flattering," she said. "Sort of like, 'well, we don't know you, and we have no reason to do this but for maybe a hint of pity, but sure, why don't you pretend you're one of us for the hell of it.'"

"Now who's the cynic?" He winked at her.

"I guess we're a great pair, aren't we?" Gisele swirled

her finger over the rim of her champagne flute, a nervous habit that was clearly an extension of her usual beer bottle label-peeling tic. "So when you're not protecting your sister's honor, what do you do?"

"By that do you mean what do I actually do, or what do I want to do?"

She toed the ground with the front of her sandals. "I didn't realize I was asking such a loaded question. Why don't you humor me? How about what do you want to do?"

"I'm not sure what you know about my family—"

"Being that we're practically related, obviously I'm completely in the know." She grinned.

"Yeah, that. In which case, you've heard that my brothers and sister and I are carrying on the tradition of Romeos from as far back as the Middle Ages in producing fine Italian wines. And because of that tradition, there is an expectation that all Romeos must follow in these footsteps and help run the family business."

"But you're like that elf who wanted to be a dentist instead of making toys."

Tomasso cocked his head and knit his brows. "Huh?"

"You know, from *Rudolph the Red-Nosed Reindeer*, that Christmas special. The song"—she held out her hands to prepare him for it, then started singing—"*Why am I such a misfit?*"

"Okay…"

She placed her hand on his shoulder. "No, I'm serious. Clearly you missed the show so I'll give you the brief rundown. Rudolph has a red nose, which means he's an outcast. He meets Hermey, an elf who hates making toys and wants to be a dentist. They set off on an epic adventure, yada yada, and they all live happily ever after once they tame the Abominable Snow Monster."

One side of Tomasso's mouth curved up into a grin. "There goes that happily ever after nonsense again."

"Of course. You can't have a Christmas special without a happy ending. Same goes for a Christmas wedding." She cocked her head. "So did you want to be a dentist, then?" She burst out laughing at her own joke.

"Um, no," he said. "Should I?"

"I'm so sorry." She shook her head. "Sometimes Parker gets mad at me because I have no filter. Which means I can be the life of the party but sometimes I blather on a bit longer than I should. Go ahead. Tell me what it is you want to do."

Tomasso glanced to either side. "I'm wondering if there is someplace we can sit down because, at this rate, it'll be midnight before I actually get a chance to speak."

Gisele frowned. "Seriously, I'll shut up." She pretended to zip her mouth shut and swallow the key, then reconsidered the gesture. "You know that never made much sense to me, swallowing the key, because your mouth is already zipped shut, right? So how would you open it to swallow the key? And then once it's swallowed, how can you ever open it again?"

Tomasso grabbed two more flutes of champagne as another tray passed them by.

"As I was saying," he said, dipping his head and looking at her as though she was nuts. "I'd rather be working with my hands. In fact, I've become quite a passionate woodworker. Before, I sort of hated every day I was stuck living a proscribed life over which I had no true control. Once I discovered the joy of this type of manual labor, I became hooked. Don't get me wrong, I have a great life. And I'm fortunate for my ancestors who built up this successful business as they have, given me the life that most would envy. The thing is, it's not that I don't like wine. Obviously I love it. I'm just sort of bored with the idea of working exclusively at Cantine dei Marchesi Romeo for the rest of my life. Instead I'm looking for something that ignites a fire in me."

Gisele eyed him from head to toe. Speaking of igniting a fire... This man was awfully easy on the eyes. And he seemed like he had a heart—at least to the extent that he wanted to honor his own wishes and desires and not simply capitulate to expectations.

"Wow," she said. "I respect you for that. Oh, wait—" She pretended to unzip her mouth and pull out the key. "Sorry, that was a joke Parker and I shared when we were kids. I am so in the habit of doing that. Okay, my mouth is unlocked now and I can go on. As I was saying, good for you, doing what speaks to your soul. You only get one life—you have to live it the way you want to."

"I'm glad you understand." He nodded. "Because the rest of my family doesn't seem to grasp it so much."

"Yeah, well, now that I'm honorary family and all, leave it to me to smooth over the ruffled feathers. At our next family gathering."

"They'll get over it." He laughed. "I know my mamma already understands. I worked so hard on the woodwork when we built our new corporate headquarters, finally she could see the fruits of my labor."

"So tell me about this passion of yours," she said, placing her hand on his. "I'd like to hear all about it."

He reached for her elbow and guided her, his hand at her back, toward an alcove with a small love seat. He motioned for her to sit down, then took the spot next to her.

"I want to be sure I'm not boring you too much," he said with a grin. "This way if you start to nod off, you won't have far to fall."

Gisele waved her hand at him. "Nonsense. I can't wait to hear about it."

"So my eldest brother Sandro, who became our surrogate father after Papà passed, had ambitious plans to build a grand headquarters for Cantine dei Marchesi Romeo wines, one that would attract tourists, a destination venue. As the plans progressed, it became even more grandiose, and the final outcome was a collaboration with the premier architects and building specialists the world over, who helped to create this gorgeous building. It's environmentally friendly, designed to blend in harmony with the landscape. Whenever possible, we used natural local resources in the building and decorating of it. It's truly a work of art in the Tuscan countryside, and the inside, *mamma mia*, it's breathtaking." He kissed his fingertips in emphasis.

Gisele had leaned forward to listen more closely. She could barely concentrate on his words, transfixed as she was with his looks, not to mention the feel of his hard legs practically pressed up next to hers. This man was so interesting, and so, well, sensual, the way his hands moved as he spoke as if they were speaking a whole different language. She tried to picture those strong, rough hands roaming her body and found herself stifling a groan.

"I'd love to see your contributions to the project," she said.

"Really?" he said. "If you're serious, my laptop is back at the palace. Maybe I can bring it over to your apartment and show you some images."

Gisele arched her brow. If this was anything like bringing his "etchings" to show her... well, she'd be totally on board. And maybe she could show him some of her own "etchings." After all, it had been far too long since she'd been up close and personal with a man.

She reached into her small clutch and found a breath mint, which she discreetly slipped into her mouth.

"I'd say now's as good a time as any." She winked, stood up, and held out her hand. It was time to see some of those images. Or better yet, make some of their own.

Chapter Two

TOMASSO Romeo was most definitely not interested in another relationship with a woman. He didn't have the time, he didn't have the interest, and he certainly didn't have the emotional energy. His crazy ex-girlfriend Liliana Brunetti had sucked the give-a-shit right out of him, and he was gun-shy. It was hard to say when he finally realized how very whacked she was, but by then the damage to his psyche had been done.

It could have been when she set up fake Facebook accounts to stalk him online after he unfriended her because she'd started bad-mouthing him on his wall, where she claimed he had a penis the size of an inchworm. It might have been when she showed up at a restaurant to spy on him—even though he was there with his cousin Isabella, who had been in Florence visiting a friend and called him last minute to meet up for drinks. Didn't help matters that she started calling Isabella—the Princess Royal of Monaforte, mind you—a dirty whore for sleeping with her man. Yeah. He wasn't sleeping with his royal cousin.

No, actually, he could pinpoint precisely when he realized he was dealing with a woman who would drive him to the brink of insanity if he didn't shake her like a baby rattle, *prontissimo*. It was when he tried to break up with her and she told him he wasn't allowed. *He wasn't allowed.* As if there were some contractual obligation to stay with a lunatic of a woman he wasn't even committed to! He'd met her on an online dating site and she was beautiful, no doubt about it. But, he learned the hard way, beauty does not equate to mental or emotional stability. They'd only dated for a month or so when he'd started trying to extricate himself from her clutches, once she demanded they see each other every single bloody damned day, though it took several long, frustrating months until he finally succeeded.

At last, a strongly worded letter from his attorney got that kook off his back once and for all, and now he was determined not to have anyone else clinging to him for the next, oh, decade or so. No, thank you. Chicks were officially off-limits. It helped that he was heading off to New York for a mentorship program in fine woodworking, and he would be too busy to deal with distractions like the opposite sex (not to mention sex itself) anyhow.

His brother Lorenzo laughed at him, warning him he couldn't go without a woman simply because he couldn't be without sex. But he took that as a challenge and became determined to prove him wrong. In fact, he went as far as making a wager with him that he could keep it in his pants at least until he returned home to Tuscany from New York. A thousand of his own hard-earned Euros were on the line, not to mention his competitive spirit: he hated losing.

That's why it was a bit unfortunate to have encountered Gisele Hornsby at such an inopportune time. Under normal circumstances, he'd be completely smitten: a sassy, girl-next-door type, with long, soft blond curls he'd already fantasized about seeing fanned across his pillows after hours of making love, because, well, he might be able to suppress the urge, but the carnal desire, not so much.

When he took one look into her bright blue eyes that afternoon as she tried to get his sister Valentina drunk so she could extract secrets from her, he felt an urgent need to pull her to him and settle his lips upon hers. At least that's what the old Tomasso would have done in a heartbeat if given the chance. But the new, improved, sexless Tomasso, decided instead to play the good guy and make sure the women got back to the palace before they did something they'd regret in their drunken state. More like before he'd do something he regretted in his blue-balled state. Because in all honesty, Gisele was gorgeous, smart, a bit of a smart-ass—and he loved a good challenge—and on top of it all, she had a banging body, and he was always a fan of a nice rack and a hot ass.

Christ, this Tomasso Romeo Chastity Challenge thing was going to kill him.

That's why he couldn't quite understand how he'd agreed to bring his laptop to Gisele's room to share pictures of his woodworking handiwork. He knew that nothing good came of late-night tête-à-têtes with hot women. But then again, this would be a great chance to test his restraint. His monk-like self-discipline was doomed to end up in self-gratification—which is never quite as good as the real thing—and would be on the chopping block if he wasn't careful.

After a sexually charged shuttle bus ride back to the palace in which his thigh pressed too comfortably to hers, and her soft, minty breath only made him fantasize about ways to get her breathing a little more anaerobically, Tomasso welcomed the break from Gisele to coach himself back to his new celibate-is-the-new-manwhore stage he'd found himself in. But once he tamped down the emerging hard-on that was still not on board with his innovative program quite yet, he firmed his resolve, grabbed his computer, and climbed the flight of stairs, navigating the labyrinthian, dark hallways of the palace, determined to be strong.

Which was how he found himself knocking on palace apartment number 11 shortly before midnight, laptop tucked beneath his armpit, ready to be neighborly and decidedly not randy.

Gisele opened the door and grabbed his wrist, quickly dragged him inside, then shut the door immediately.

"What was that for?" he said, pulling his hand away from her grasp—the less physical contact, the better. She seemed embarrassed to have him show up or something, which was uncalled for.

"Sorry. I didn't want anyone getting the wrong idea, what with you appearing up here like this. My brother would kill me if he thought I was entertaining a man at this hour, and, well, since he's not back, I just thought it would be best to be a little careful is all."

"If you'd rather I leave—." He held up his hands in surrender.

"Oh, gosh, no," she said. "I'm honestly excited to see your stuff."

Good God, if only he could see *her* stuff, he'd be pretty damned stoked too. But he needed to fulfill his pledge: he could refrain from making a shameless play at a gorgeous woman for once in his life. He mentally repeated his mantra: Monk-like restraint. Monk-like restraint.

"And I'm excited to show it to you."

If only he could *show it to her*. The mere thought erected

a tentpole in his pants. Curse those autonomic reflexes. He tried to will his burgeoning cock into submission, thinking about anything that would tamp down his evidently uncontrollable sexual urges. What about that raccoon he saw flattened on the road the other day? Ugh, no. Raccoons have those peculiar masks over their eyes, and that immediately reminded him of the totally hot stripper who was naked but for a mask strapped to her face at Luca's stag party last week. That thought only made things worse. Hmmm, how about thinking of how pissed Lorenzo would be when he had to pony up once he lost the bet. Firm resolve is what he needed. He could do it. Now to get his Johnson on board with that.

Gisele settled into the overstuffed leather sofa in the living room and patted the empty spot next to her. "Have a seat. Make yourself comfortable."

Comfortable would be lifting the hem of that hot dress of hers and slipping aside the black lace panties he'd fantasized were beneath it and sliding his cock into her warm body.

Fuck. This is going to be harder than I expected. Just as absence makes the heart grow fonder, abstinence seemed to make the cock grow harder.

"Why don't I set it up here on the kitchen counter?"

"Thanks, but I'm super comfy on this sofa." She rubbed the leather. "I can't believe how buttery soft it feels. I'm such a tactile person. I love natural things like down comforters or leather furniture that envelope me in comfort."

Which got him to thinking: if he had her naked on her hands and knees and took her from behind, he could envelop her in his body. He wondered if that would be tactile enough for her.

"Uh," he said, worrying that gibberish was all that was going to slip from his lips at this point. Gisele had stretched out her long, shapely legs, resting her feet with those sexy-as-hell sandals on the glass coffee table.

"C'mon over. Don't be a stranger." She curled her finger to motion him over. "I promise I won't bite."

But could he promise he wouldn't bite? Or lick. Or nibble. Or suck.

Willpower, man.

"Sure," he said, as he walked to the sofa like a man headed to the gallows and settled himself down next to her. He'd removed his tie and suit jacket back in his apartment, unbuttoning his shirt at the collar and rolling up his sleeves. Perhaps it would have been wiser to don a parka, maybe a pair of ski pants. He opened his laptop and booted it up.

"Oh, look how pretty it is out there." Gisele pointed to the wall of windows; beyond them a gentle snow had started to fall, the dappled flakes making the cityscape seem like an Impressionist painting. "I can't believe how amazing this apartment is."

"Not a bad place to spend some time, is it?" He smiled.

"Are you kidding? I've been to some incredible places in my life, but this takes the cake." She lifted a finger. "Speaking of cake, I picked up some dessert at a small patisserie when we were in town today. Would you like a some?"

Dessert was a brilliant idea: anything to occupy his hands and mouth right now would be a welcome diversion.

"I'd love that. In fact, why don't you stay put and I'll serve us since you're comfortable already." Keeping his distance would let him control himself a bit better. "Just direct me to the goods and I've got you covered." Although what he'd like to cover her with was his bare flesh, but that was so not in the cards.

He brought out two glasses of water and a plate with several French macarons with chocolate ganache filling, and placed them on the coffee table, right next to her slender, strong legs. He closed his eyes until he could redirect his attention from the dessert he wanted to the dessert he was stuck with. When Gisele took a bite of the colorful confection, she groaned, which so distracted Tomasso as he chomped down on his, he squeezed the chocolate ganache right out of the center of his macaron onto his white button-down.

"Oh, goodness, look at you," Gisele said, staring at the brown icing staining his chest. "Here, let me get that off you so I can treat this before the stain sets."

"No, no. It's fine. Really." He held up his hands, resisting.

"But I insist," she said as she reached to unbutton his shirt. "I have this great stuff that will take the stain right out. But it has to be treated immediately." She continued to release the buttons from the placket, and despite himself, Tomasso was powerless to stop her.

"There," she said after loosening the final button. "If you'll let me slip this off." She pulled first one sleeve down, then the other, leaving a bare-chested Tomasso with what had officially become the girl of his dreams practically drooling over the sight of him. It turned him on more than he could have ever imagined.

He was so fucked.

Chapter Three

HOLY mackerel! There was no way she could resist this guy sitting deliciously half-naked in front of her. One glance at his very bare and very strong broad shoulders and upper torso, sprinkled with the right amount of hair to run curious fingers through, and she knew she had to have a piece of him. She hadn't even dared let her gaze drop farther down his body yet. Too bad that ganache didn't spill right there, or she'd have probably up and licked it off him, no questions asked. Which perhaps would be a little too sexually aggressive, considering they'd only met ten hours earlier.

"I'll just be a sec."

She went back to her toiletry bag in the bathroom and grabbed a stain stick, put a washcloth beneath the shirt to absorb the fluid, and began to dab. It took a few minutes, but before she knew it, the smear of chocolate had dissipated so much she could barely see it.

As she returned to the living room, she couldn't help but notice that Tomasso's lap seemed a bit fuller than it had been a few minutes ago.

Ohmigod. He wants me as much as I want him. This could get interesting.

She draped his shirt over the back of a bar stool in the

kitchen. "We should let that dry for a bit. If you're cold I can get you something of my brother's to borrow."

She tried to come up with some quick-thinking excuse about how all of his shirts must be in the laundry because there wasn't a one to be found. No way was she going to cover up such perfect scenery if she could help it.

"I guess I'll be okay."

Much to her chagrin, as soon as he heard her approach, he quickly moved the computer to his lap, covering up the evidence of his arousal, and began scrolling through images. Hmmm. On second thought, maybe he wasn't here for those "etchings" after all but had truly planned to show her his stuff. Gisele hoped this was merely his version of foreplay.

She plunked down next to him and offered him another cookie. He lifted his water glass and chugged a gulp down. "Now at least you don't have to worry about food stains," she said. "I mean, next spill, you can just lick it off."

He choked on his water, and she reflexively reached to pat his back, which felt oh so good, her hand pressed to his skin.

Did she just say that? She was eternally grateful she hadn't offered to lick it herself. Which, obviously would be her instinctual reaction. Her brother was always grousing about her lack of impulse control.

"I guess," he said in a resigned-sounding voice.

Gisele decided she needed to back off or she might scare the guy.

"Ooh, so these are things you've made?"

He perked up immediately. "Yes, as I was saying earlier, these are some of the things I worked on at the Romeo headquarters."

He regaled her with a slideshow of various wood panels of relief carvings depicting the grape harvest, boar hunting, and other typically Tuscan scenes.

"I have to tell you, I thought you were going to show me like a set of stairs you built or something." She pointed at the screen. "But this stuff, these are amazing works of art. You've carved all these intricate scenes and animals and mythical creatures, and all using local wood. This is unbelievable. You're truly an artist."

Tomasso beamed. "It's what I love to do."

"But your family frowns upon it?"

He grimaced. "It's complicated. The thing is everyone in my family has always been expected to do the family business."

"Which is wine."

He nodded. "That's almost an understatement. We're the largest producer of wine in Tuscany and our wines have been the favorites of kings, diplomats, and even your average wine snobs for hundreds and hundreds of years. I'm not sure if anyone has ever defied the family mandate to do their own thing." He continued to scroll through the images, pointing out particular favorites as he went. "My mamma is very proud of me and she's now encouraging me to 'follow my bliss'—her words—but my brothers aren't particularly thrilled with me. They want me to bear part of the burden of Romeo wines."

Gisele removed the ponytail holder from her braid and freed her hair, running her fingers through it to get the kinks out. She leaned in closer to look at his photographs, her blond hair draping over his hard stomach. She could hear his sharp intake of breath.

"I may have mentioned—I don't have a huge family, so

maybe I can't relate to pressure to conform to family expectations. Perhaps that makes me a bit biased." She leaned in more as she scrolled across the screen, staring intently at his work. "But I gotta tell you, it would be a waste of your gifts if you didn't pursue this and see where it took you."

He knit his brows. "Honestly? You're not just being polite?"

"God, no. These are lost arts you have captured beautifully. The world needs people like you to provide such beauty, a counterpart to the mundane world in which most of us live. I don't doubt you're a perfectly good vintner or accountant or marketing whiz, whatever it is Romeo wines needs you to be, but I'd imagine with your gigantic family, there are others who can do that equally as well. The world probably needs another wine expert far less than it needs someone who can brighten our lives with works of art."

She looked up at him, only to find his face mere inches from hers.

"Has anyone told you that you have the most beautiful eyes?" He pinned her with an intense gaze as he leaned in closer still. "Something about them pulls me in, in much the same way that working with wood somehow calls to me."

Gisele froze in place, unable to think of a proper response to his comment. But the idea of working with his wood sure called to her. Her hands were tired from leaning on them while she looked at his computer screen, but she didn't dare move an inch. The heater turned on and the blast of warmth forced air where they sat, making the tips of her hair dance across his chest. Tomasso groaned.

He tucked a strand of her hair behind her ear, then

placed his hand beneath her chin, gently pulling her toward him. "Nothing personal, but something tells me I'm going to regret this."

Chapter Four

WHAT. The. Fuck. Was. He. Doing?

This very thought played on a dueling loop that ran through Tomasso's brain, right along with the notion of how much he wanted to feel that blond hair of hers on his thighs as she settled between them, her mouth over his hard cock. Alas, thought number two won, and he could not stop himself from acting on his impulses as he inhaled the fresh, citrusy smell of her shampoo and settled his lips over hers. She released a tiny sigh as their lips merged, and he couldn't help but run his tongue along the seam of hers, urging her to open to his overtures. With his free hand, he shifted his laptop discreetly onto the coffee table, hoping there would be no more need for what he now realized was merely a prop for his inevitable intentions. Who was he to think he could go without this?

Tomasso ran his fingers through her hair as his tongue traced encouraging strokes along hers. She moaned, and he reached a hand behind her, cupping her curvy ass and pulling her on top of him, his hard length fitting the perfect notch between her legs. It was his turn to moan. He pressed her bottom toward him so there was no mistaking his desires, and she rolled her hips against his hardness and deepened the kiss as her hands skirted over his shoulders, his arms, and his chest. If he thought his dick couldn't get any harder, he was sorely mistaken, and he felt it throb against his fly while Gisele ground into him. It had been months since he'd been with a woman and he was jumping out of his skin with the need to touch her, to feel her warm and wet and wanting.

His hands coasted along her bare back and desperate to feel more of her, he slid his fingers, beneath the spaghetti straps, gently tugging them off her shoulders, then following the top edge of the dress in search of the zipper. He tugged it and the dress gave way as if it had been in on the conspiracy to get her out of it all along. Quickly, he pulled it over her head, tossing it carelessly onto the floor and leaving her naked but for those sexy-as-fuck sandals and red lace thong; it left little to the imagination and surpassed the black one he'd envisioned. He tried to take a deep breath to settle down the urgent, carnal needs that were overwhelming his senses, but it was impossible. This woman had gotten under his skin despite himself and he needed more. Now.

Once he'd freed her from the confines of the dress, he flipped her onto her back on the sofa, taking charge to gain better access, pressing his solid body to her soft one, flesh to flesh at last. He dipped his head in search of a breast, and his mouth quickly fastened on her hard nipple, licking and sucking and nipping at it till she panted with need.

"Ohhh, Tomasso." She breathed heavily as she pressed his head to her breast. "Don't stop. That feels fucking amazing."

She fumbled for his belt, deftly pulling it from the belt loop and unfastening it in swift, skillful motions. She unbuttoned his pants, slipping the zipper of his fly down, and slid her hand beneath the waistband of his boxer briefs, finally releasing his cock from the fabric confinement that was about killing him. But then she coiled her warm fingers around his hardness and he thought he'd not last another minute.

"*Cara mia*," he said on a groan. "*Di più*. More."

He pressed rough woodworker hands beneath the flimsy edge of her thong, sliding his fingers over her smooth skin, slipping with ease to her wet center. Gisele gasped, thrusting her hips toward his talented fingers as they parted and stroked along her swollen pussy.

"Oh, my God, Tomasso, you are so gifted with your hands." He picked up the pace, circling her clit while he suckled her breast. He could feel her body tense as she shouted out his name yet again, her muscles quivering as she locked his hands on her thighs, grinding herself toward his fingers.

After momentarily catching her breath, Gisele urged Tomasso onto his back as she sat on her haunches, admiring the near-perfect specimen of maleness: his strong, broad shoulders, his well-developed pecs, and a cut stomach that served as the red-carpet pathway to the main event: his gorgeous, gigantic cock. She leaned forward and swiped her tongue along the base of his throat, then trailed it across his chest, paying close attention to first one nipple, then the other while her hand stroked his hard length.

She continued licking her way down his body, swirling her tongue around his navel, and following the trail of dark hair that beckoned until she found the Holy Grail. She pressed her tongue to the tip and licked in small strokes, slowly working down the tip and around his cock like he was her own personal lollipop.

Tomasso groaned out loud right as she opened her mouth and slowly took the girth of him inside. She moaned as her lips enveloped him, knowing the vibrations would drive him even more crazy. She took him as deep as she could then slowly released him, pulling him in again, sucking hard this time.

She almost didn't hear the sounds of someone approaching, but thankfully she did: the jangling of keys, the press of footsteps coming down the hallway.

Survival instincts kicked in suddenly and she sat up fast. "My brother. Shit. Get up. Now!"

She was off Tomasso in the blink of an eye, quickly throwing her dress back on while ordering him to zip up his pants.

"Crap. We need to hide you." She rapidly gathered up his laptop and collected the mess from their dessert, hoping to destroy any evidence that would point toward his presence. "My brother is super protective of me. He'd kill me if he knew you were here."

She shooed him down toward her room and into the bathroom, forcing him into the private toilet stall and closing the door.

She glanced in the mirror, hoping to erase all signs of having just orgasmed her way to happytown, then fluffed her hair to tamp down any obvious disarray. "You stay here," she said as if talking to a naughty dog. She raced to the front hallway and placed her ear to the door listening for signs of imminent intrusion by her brother, but hearing nothing more. After waiting a few beats, she gingerly opened the door and poked her head out, glancing down the hall in one direction and then the other, seeing not a soul. Relieved, she shut the door and hurried back to the bedroom.

"Pssst," she said as she opened the door to the bathroom to find him awkwardly standing atop the toilet. "Hurry. Coast is clear, temporarily at least. You have to leave, now."

Poor Tomasso stared, dumbfounded.

"I know. Sorry to leave you hanging like that but I can't take a chance. Now come on." She grabbed his hand and tugged. "Let's get you out of her, fast."

And in a complete reversal of the manner in which she greeted him hardly more than an hour earlier, she opened the door, double-checked that the coast was indeed clear, and pushed poor Tomasso out the door before he could even attempt a protest.

At times like this, she wished like hell she didn't have to worry about what other people thought, because, damn, that was one unforgettable time until the threat of Parker had to go and ruin it. As much as she'd have loved to take this lovely little episode to its expected conclusion, no way was she going to risk the wrath—and reprimand—of her big brother. She was supposed to be on her best behavior at this wedding. And, like it or not, best behavior meant not having sex with the cousin of the groom.

Chapter Five

TOMASSO knew he'd dodged a bullet during that episode with Gisele. *That episode*. As if. More like that un-fucking-believably hot almost-sex with the most gorgeous woman he'd been cut off by in, well, ever. He couldn't believe it was she who left him with a bad case of blue balls and not the other way around. Rather than adhering to the moral code he'd firmly established, he'd gone completely in the opposite direction. What the hell? How could he be so incapable of avoiding sexual encounters? At least he hadn't technically welshed on the bet yet. Since the act wasn't completed, he could remain guilt-free. He hadn't officially broken his vow. Perhaps it was a matter of semantics, but he wasn't going to quibble with it and luckily Lorenzo would be none the wiser.

He'd have been fine if only it weren't for her damned hair, draped around him like a privacy fence obscuring what she was doing to him so only he could watch, mesmerized. Oh, and those sandals he kept fantasizing about.

He truly didn't want to get involved with any damned woman, but she seemed sweet and interested in him, not the prestige of his family, unlike Liliana, and he hadn't hooked up for a while, and well, there they were alone: two grown adults and those sandals. Even now, he could barely erase the idea of stripping her down to nothing more than those hot heels, maybe taking her from behind while she wore them.

This would serve as a cautionary tale and he'd keep his damned distance from that temptress. Clearly she held some magical sway over his ability to keep his dick in his pants.

He felt the need to simply lay it all out there with Gisele, let her know that whatever this thing was simmering like a mirage in the desert between them could never go further. Especially because he was that starving man crawling across the hot sand and that made her all the more alluring to him. He grabbed for his phone and dialed her number, which she'd shared with him at the party last night.

Her voice was so damned chipper when she answered, he felt awful about the reason behind the call.

"Hey," he said, his voice coming out more like a grunt.

"Hey, yourself. Whatcha got going on today?"

"Getting together with school friends, that sort of thing." He wasn't about to tell her he planned to quarantine himself in his apartment in the palace rather than show up at any event that involved hiding from whatever was brewing between them. He could only sequester himself from her so much over the next few days. He'd have to pick his battles wisely. With any luck, he could at the very least dodge her till the prewedding gala dinner, maybe even find himself a camouflage tuxedo to wear to the wedding, to keep him incognito from dangerous enticements like Gisele.

"I was hoping we could maybe meet up, go into town for a little while."

Tomasso balled his hands into fists. This would not be as easy as he'd hoped. "Yeah. Sorry. I have a full schedule. Won't be available much at all."

"How about if we sit together during the sleigh ride tomorrow?"

"Actually I don't think that's going to work out. I've got something else going on."

"Okay, then," she said. "Um, well, good luck with that."

"Thanks." He wiped sweat from his palms onto his pants, feeling like such a complete asshole ditching her like this. But it was for the best. "Take care."

"I'll be sure to." With that, she hung up, no good-bye.

Well, that went well. He ran his fingers through his hair, feeling like such a heel for letting her down so hard. Under other circumstances, maybe they could have pursued what was obviously a mutual attraction. But now was not the time and he'd have to leave it at that.

Wow. What a complete asshole! He was none too happy to get in my pants last night and now he's acting as if he barely knows me, let alone wants to spend a minute with me.

Gisele could feel her temper simmering to a slow boil, but she was determined not to let it get the best of her. She was still at a palace for a wedding, so she simply had to keep things in perspective. She didn't need that man in her life, and she truly didn't know him enough to care. If he wasn't interested in her, that was his problem.

She could ignore him right back and then some. Which

ended up being much easier than expected, since he failed to show up at that evening's reception and again for the sleigh ride the following day. At first, she'd gotten her hopes up when she saw a tall, dark-haired, brown-eyed man who looked deceivingly like Tomasso, but it turned out to be his brother Lorenzo. Just as well. She had no interest in spending time with the Romeo brothers; she was perfectly content to hang with Valentina and to hell with the male faction of that family.

She knew, however, she'd likely run into him at the prewedding gala dinner, which Valentina said was a slightly less formal version of a wedding reception. For the royals, that meant perhaps not as many official-type uniforms, maybe not so many swords and cords and badges and medals dangling from elaborately decorated military costumes. She had to believe they were costumes and not actual functional uniforms, because what military man could wear those things on a battlefield and not sink into the mud and drown from the very weight of the garments alone? She tried not to imagine what Tomasso would look like in one of those. Or better still in a tuxedo. She'd have a hard time resisting him in that.

Gisele had loved the opportunity to dress up for the many royal nuptial events this week. At home, a pair of jeans, heels, and a slouchy sweater were about as fancy as she got when going out. More often than not, she could be found in yoga pants and a sweatshirt and a pair of Uggs. But this, well, this was license to pretend she was a princess of sorts, and she had taken advantage of it.

She and Valentina had spent the afternoon getting ready for the prewedding gala dinner, with the full barrage of primping such an occasion would merit. They had manis and pedis followed by hair and makeup styling done by professionals. Even though she got the important things out of the way in advance, it took Gisele a good hour to get ready for the event. She went all out with her chosen gown: a slinky off-the-shoulder satin and silk body-hugging Armani number in midnight blue.

She took a final look in the mirror before departing for the event, glanced over her shoulder to see how she looked from the back, and gave herself an assenting nod. While she hoped that stupid Tomasso would eat his heart out when and if she had the chance to see him, in reality, she was dressing to please herself, not some man she'd never see again. And she was pleased with how beautiful she looked and felt.

Parker had arranged for a limo to take the three of them to the venue. When they arrived at the National Gallery and debarked from their stretch SUV limousine, Gisele felt as if they were equally important royal guests. And while there was one guest she sort of—if she had to admit it—wanted to see tonight, in truth, if she never saw Tomasso again, she'd be fine with that. She didn't need a useless man to make her feel special.

Chapter Six

TOMASSO took one look at Gisele in that body-hugging gown that fell off her shoulders, practically inviting him to pull it down the rest of the way, and knew he'd have a hell of a time steering clear of her. With hair pulled back and off her shoulders and soft blond tendrils framing her face, she looked like an angel—one with a devilishly talented mouth, if his fleeting firsthand experience of the other night was any indication.

He'd been watching for her as she entered through the gallery's grand entrance, and she did indeed make an entrance befitting the venue, looking elegant and sexy and truly more beautiful than any woman in the place. He was used to the type of women who wore their importance like a badge of honor, who dressed to impress and whose attire and makeup and general presentation were a sort of suit of armor announcing how imperious they were. But here was Gisele, looking a bit girlish and awkward, certainly adorable, yet sensual, and all of it seemed natural. Nothing about her screamed "look at me" like those many women who wanted only that.

It made him rethink what now seemed like an ill-conceived plan to avoid entanglements with women. *Why would I want to steer clear of that?* he wondered as his eyes practically ingested her from head to toe. Maybe contrary to his current mode of thinking, all women weren't created equal, and perhaps some were worth a second glance.

He hurriedly made his way toward the entryway to get a closer look, maybe even have a chance to explain himself a bit better to her. As Tomasso hastened in that direction, navigating through a throng of guests, he knocked into an elderly man in a formal kilt, spilling his bourbon all over the man's jacket and apron. In his haste, he barely stopped to apologize, tossing his handkerchief to him to dab it dry, waving apologies as he continued forward. Finally he came face-to-face with Gisele.

She squinted her eyes at him, nodding curtly. "Tomasso."

"*Cara*," he said, reaching for her hand and pulling it to his lips for a soft kiss. "You look absolutely breathtaking."

"Gee, thanks." She pulled her hand back and turned away from him, trying to catch Parker's attention. But her brother was completely engrossed in conversation as he walked into the crowd with a proprietary hand at the base of Valentina's back. The sight made Tomasso wistful that he wasn't doing that at this very moment with the woman standing before him. Gisele sighed deeply, her eyes obviously scanning the crowd for anyone other than Tomasso with whom she could feign compelling conversation.

"Look, Gisele—" he said, furrowing his brow, trying to figure out how to explain away his perceived indifference to her, even as he wanted nothing more than to grab her hand again and not only kiss it, but lick it all the way up her arm, making a path toward her mouth.

She shook her head. "It's okay, Tomasso. You don't

owe me an explanation. The whole thing was sort of impulsive and strange anyhow, and honestly, I regretted it as much as you obviously did. Let's leave it at that—no big deal. We'll never see each other again, so it's all good."

With that, she turned and slipped away into the throng, and he didn't choose to pursue her. Sure, he felt bad about it, but he had to do what was right for him, even if it might be the worst decision he'd made in a long time.

Despite a rough start with that regrettable Tomasso pretending he gave a care about her, Gisele had a lovely time at the dinner, laughing and chatting with several charming guests seated near her, including a count and a countess, a diplomatic attaché, and a woman who was in charge of the palace dogs, of all things.

After dinner, she danced with more old men wearing sashes and medals than she ever thought she'd see in her life. It was a royalty thing, and she eventually started having sash envy. That and tiara envy. How fun would that be to sport some diamond-and-sapphire-encrusted tiara, looking like Audrey Hepburn? She decided next time she was heading to some dull fundraiser in Manhattan, she would find herself one to wear—at least there she'd not appear as a poseur with one crowning her head.

At last she was ready to call it a night. Her feet hurt, her heart, or maybe just her feelings sort of ached a little, and she needed to be alone. As she started working her way through the large crowd, Tomasso approached her.

"Can I have a word with you?" He reached for her elbow to stop her forward momentum.

She glared at him. "Actually, I was just leaving." She kept trying to maneuver away from him, but there seemed to be bodies blocking her way no matter which direction she went.

"Gisele," he said, pausing as if trying to figure out what he was going to say. "I wanted to apologize for any misunderstandings."

She arched a brow. "Trust me, there were no misunderstandings, Tomasso. I read you loud and clear. Now if you'll let me get by—"

"But—"

Only she found a gap in the throng and quickly slipped away, leaving Tomasso to stare after her, his face a mask of frustration.

Tomasso wasn't used to being the bad guy and it didn't sit well with him at all. He felt an urgent need to set things straight so that Gisele didn't think badly of him. It seemed the gentlemanly thing to do.

He decided the only way to achieve this would be to stop by her room on the way back to his own apartment, once back at the palace. He navigated his way down the tricky corridors of the palace until he came to apartment 11, and knocked gently.

After a minute, Gisele opened the door and stood before him still in that seductive dress that made him want to bite down on his arm to avoid pulling at the thing to once again see her beautiful body on full display. Damn, he was a conflicted soul.

She cocked her head sideways and crossed her arms, not even bothering to say anything to him.

"Look, I owe you an explanation." He leaned on the doorframe. "May I please come in?"

She rolled her eyes. "Fine. But don't plan on sticking around. Parker's busy doing God knows what with your sister, but he'll be back at some point and the last thing I need is for him to be under the deeply erroneous impression that you are anything to me. It's one thing if he presumed that and he was right, but I'm not about to take heat from him for a big fat nothing."

Gisele motioned for Tomasso to enter, then closed the door behind him.

He made the mistake of glancing at her breasts, on full display in that clingy gown. He took a deep breath.

"So the thing is—" he turned his head away and looked down.

She squinted at him. "Are you about to get sick or something?"

He let out a laugh. "My God, no," he said. "Anything but." Lust sick might be more like it.

She let out a big yawn, covering her mouth with her hand. "Then how about you cut to the chase. I'm pretty beat."

Crap. He'd made a mess of things here. He looked at her mouth, her soft pink lips, and he wanted nothing more than to place his own lips on them, close his eyes, and block out the rest of the world while he paced his breathing to hers and followed those animalistic cues that men and women do when they're drawn to one another.

"Can we sit down?"

"I don't see the point in that. Surely you can say what you need to say here."

He slipped his hand in hers and ushered her to the sofa. The same sofa that was the scene of their near coupling a few nights earlier. The same beautiful sofa on which… Forget it. He had to put what happened out of his mind. He needed to figure out what he should even say to her. He had no fucking clue at this point.

"So the other night—"

"Really, I'd just as soon not discuss that."

"But I owe you an explanation."

"Let's pretend it didn't happen and then you can leave and I'll go to sleep and all will be right with the world."

"But see that's not how it should be." He turned toward her. "Please, won't you sit?"

"Fine. Whatever." She shrugged and plunked herself down dramatically.

He took a seat next to her, then turned to face her. "I'm truly sorry if I hurt your feelings, Gisele."

She frowned at him but said nothing.

He continued. "I think you're nice and interesting and fun and beautiful."

"Of course. That's how it is with men like you. You'll lie and say whatever you want to get what you want, and then—"

He shook his head vigorously. "You've got it all wrong."

"Trust me, it's not the first time some guy has led me

on to get down my pants, only to have a change of heart." She stared off into the dark city outside. "Look, it was fun while it lasted. Believe me, I'm not going to suffer emotional trauma from this or anything."

But Tomasso had tuned her out, mesmerized with the subtle fringe of violet that ringed her blue irises and the rose hue of her full lips and that creamy white skin of her shoulders. What the hell was he thinking turning someone like this down?

"The thing is, Gisele, I found you compelling from the moment I met you when you were trying to get my sister drunk so she'd spill her secrets about why she hated your brother. And then the other night, when you were interested in me, not who I was, well, that was quite a refreshing change from what I'm used to. And then God, when you kissed me—"

"When *I* kissed *you?*" She raised her voice as she addressed him. "That's some revisionist history, buster. That was all on you."

"Gah!" He threw his arms up in exasperation. "Try as I might, I can't put this into words."

He leaned forward and put his hands on either side of her face, pulling her toward him.

"I find you horribly irresistible," he said as he settled his lips on hers. But she was having none of it and pursed her lips against his attempt at a kiss. He dragged his tongue along the seam of her mouth, determined to let her know that—like it or not—he was indeed attracted to her.

"Well, I'm finding you entirely *re*sistible." She pushed him away.

"Dammit, Gisele, I'm trying to tell you it's not you, it's me. If there weren't all sorts of extenuating circumstances,

I'd happily pursue whatever this crazy chemistry is between us."

"Trust me, the only chemistry between us is the kind where you mix two volatile elements together and it creates something smelly and toxic."

"I'd say it's more like the sort of chemistry that creates fireworks that blaze a trail across the night sky."

"No, I'd suggest, say, an oxidation reaction that leads to rust. Or fermentation that leaves a sour aroma that lingers for hours. Like rancid sauerkraut."

He winced at being compared to fetid food. Rarely had his ego taken such a hit. "So enough with the chemistry allegory. Clearly that backfired." He placed his hands on her shoulders, his fingers teasing the edge of her off-the-shoulder sleeves. "I'd love if you could give me a second chance. I was despondent watching you dance with all those men earlier tonight."

"Oh, you mean the octogenarian who could barely stand, the one who made me place my hands atop his on the walker for stability? Or perhaps the elderly gentleman with the ear horn? Who knew anyone still used them?" She grinned.

He dragged the tip of his finger from the edge of her mouth upward, as if drawing a smile. "That's what I like to see, that beautiful smile."

He pulled her toward him, again settling his lips on hers. This time she seemed more receptive.

"Something about you makes me feel a little crazy," he said, toying with her sleeves as he deepened the kiss, his tongue swirling around her still somewhat reluctant one. Slowly he slipped her sleeves down till her breasts were almost all the way out of her bodice. Tomasso groaned.

His lifted his mouth, seeking the crest of her breasts with his hungry lips.

"God, Gisele," he said. "I shouldn't be doing this. But I can't help myself."

She sat up, pushing him away. "What do you mean you shouldn't be doing this? I thought this was some sort of apology tour, where you were coming groveling back to get into my good graces."

"Yes, I wanted to apologize," he said, combing his fingers through his head, his stupid suddenly responsible brain having pinned down his irresponsible cock that had been steering the conversation for the past ten minutes. "I feel awful for how I've behaved."

"Yet you're trying for a command performance as you pave the way to bail again. That is so uncool."

"Look, Gisele. It's complicated. I can't do relationships right now."

"Fine! Then don't do relationships! But don't try to woo me and come on to me like you're on board with me, happy to get me naked so you can have your way, then backpedal yourself right out the door once you're satisfied. Thanks, but no thanks."

"You don't understand."

"I don't, nor do I want to. I think it's time you leave."

"But, but, but, I promise you—it's nothing personal. I just can't have that in my life right now. It was a moment of weakness. It's hard to resist someone like you. I mean I like dogs a lot, too, but I can't handle the burden of a dog in my life either."

Gisele's eyes widened. "Woof," she said, throwing him a deadpan look. "I never thought of myself as a burden before. Or a dog, for that matter. Thanks a ton for that. Oh,

and PS: you're lucky I don't slap you right now, Tomasso Romeo." She tugged up her sleeves and crossed her hands at her chest, assuring he had absolutely no parting view of her cleavage. "You know where the door is. Use it."

With that she stood and stormed off to her bedroom, slamming the door behind her.

Chapter Seven

"SO it's been over a week since we've been back from Europe, and still you seem to have this edge about you," Parker said to Gisele over beers at a new microbrewery on the Upper West Side. "What gives?"

Gisele shook her head. "What do you mean, what gives?"

Her brother shrugged. "Oh, I guess it's because normally you're bubbly and vivacious and cheerful and optimistic and since we've gotten back, you've been a bit grumpy and seem like you're dragging your feet around like a sullen child."

She half laughed. "A sullen child? You're going to pull that one out again?"

After their mother died and Gisele had kind of shut down, mired in sadness, Parker invoked the "sullen child" accusation because, for some reason, it made her laugh. Perhaps because she was rarely if ever that sort of person growing up. Gisele was the little girl who would reach out to the lonely kid on the playground everyone else ignored. The one who brought a flower to her teacher because she knew it would make her smile. She made cupcakes for girlfriends when their boyfriends ditched them. Sullen wasn't in her repertoire. Even now, really.

"Honestly, Parker. I appreciate your concern, but there's nothing wrong with me."

She failed to mention that there was plenty wrong with that chickenshit Tomasso guy, who was happy to light a fire under her but promptly extinguished it with his own pathetic protestations. So, yeah, she was still dwelling on that. It wasn't fair and it made her angry and she felt like she didn't get the final word, which bugged her. She wanted to tell him what she thought of his cowardly ways, but, well, she was a guest at that wedding and she had to keep her mouth shut in deference to her brother. Not like she even had a chance at the actual wedding. The man avoided her as if she would infect him with some sort of communicable disease if he came near her. Which was fine with her. She had a perfectly lovely time at the wedding without him. Besides, she didn't want to give Parker any ammunition to use against her, and if he knew about the whole Tomasso mess, it would surely backfire and lead to all sorts of teasing and reminders of her embarrassing debacle. He was still giving her grief for meddling with Valentina. She'd rather keep it to herself and stew a bit longer.

"Maybe it's just the winter doldrums," she said. "I mean, all that December snow was glorious and romantic in Monaforte, but now in January, it's sort of dirty and slushy and makes you cold and wet and cranky."

"I guess that means you don't want to go off on a ski holiday then?"

She rolled her eyes. "About as much as I'd love to have voluntary dental surgery. Thanks, but no thanks. Wake me when spring gets here, would ya?" Normally she loved to ski, but she was kind of tired of feeling cold and dreary. "Now if you have any interest in a long weekend in the

Caribbean, let me know. But meanwhile, what about you? You've been mooning about like an old, sad cow. Seems like absence from Valentina isn't doing you any huge favors." She swore he'd spent his waking hours FaceTiming with the woman.

He sighed. "I'd be lying if I said I didn't miss her. Funny how you can know someone and never miss them. Then you happen upon them again and bam, you're no longer yourself without them nearby."

"Ahh, love." Gisele scrunched her nose. *Love schmove.* She didn't have much interest in that sappy crapola.

Parker wagged his finger at her. "You may mock me now, but in time you'll find yourself feeling this way about someone."

She took a sip of her beer, then feigned filing her fingernails and yawning. "Yeah. Wake me when that happens."

"Such a cynic you've become." He sliced some cheese from the charcuterie platter they'd ordered, stacking it with a piece of prosciutto onto a slice of baguette. "When did my baby sister become so jaded?"

She sighed. "I'm not jaded. I'm simply not in the mood for a man."

"I'm sorry," Parker said. "Obviously something happened to sour you. Here's hoping someone even better will come along to sweeten you back up." He tipped his mug of beer to hers, then gently squeezed her cheek affectionately.

She'd successfully dodged discussing whatever did—or didn't—happen with Tomasso in the early predawn hours before the wedding. She was being the good girl by playing it straight, not letting on about how annoyed she was with

Tomasso and instead remaining coy. But now that the royal wedding was over and done, he was out of her mind for good. *Arrivederci*, sucker. She'd officially washed her hands of Tomasso once and for all.

Tomasso couldn't stop thinking about what a complete idiot he'd been with Gisele that night at the palace. It was bad enough he'd gone back groveling, only to get a bad case of the guilts in the middle of it all and essentially withdrawing his overtures. What a dunce. But then to linger in her apartment, hoping she'd reconsider and open her locked door, come out to the living room and discuss things like two sane adults? That was nothing short of nuts.

Clearly she was the sane one and he was crazy as a loon. Because then he went and nodded off on the sofa, falling asleep until near dawn. As he snuck out of her apartment, who did he run into yet again but Parker, also trying to feign innocence. Yeesh. He only hoped Parker didn't recount to Gisele what had occurred between them because he had no doubt Gisele would show up at his door and smack him one. She had a little feistiness to her, which meant that would be entirely unsurprising behavior. He was banking on Parker not wanting to let Gisele know he had been out until dawn.

Since returning home to Italy before leaving for his upcoming apprenticeship in the States, he'd tried to get Gisele out of his head, but with little success. Instead he moped around the palace like a pouty child, lamenting the mistakes he'd made. His sister was getting wise to him.

"Honestly, Tomasso, if I didn't know you better, I'd say you were pining away for a girl, the way you're grumping around this place. You even yelled at Allegra this morning. That's not like you," Valentina said as she sliced open a cornetto at the breakfast table and spread marmalade on it.

"You yelled at Allegra?" his older brother Lorenzo said. "What the hell? That's like beating up your grandmother."

Allegra had been like a nanny to the Romeo children, and although they were grown up now, she lived with the family and helped out as needed, serving breakfast and cooking many of the large family meals.

Tomasso held his hands up in surrender. "I didn't yell at her. I asked her strongly where the hell was my espresso."

Valentina rolled her eyes. "Way to come off as a pretentious git. You owe her an apology for that."

"Or I'll force you to do so," Lorenzo said, hovering over him in an imposing stance.

"Who's forcing whom to do what?" a voice said from around the corner. It was their mamma, Fabiana, a beautiful woman with short, no-nonsense salt-and-pepper hair and warm brown eyes.

As she took her seat, Allegra entered with Tomasso's espresso. Valentina and Lorenzo glared at him.

"Okay, fine," Tomasso said, looking up at Allegra with puppy dog eyes. "I'm sorry I snarled at you. I didn't mean to be rude. I'm distracted."

Allegra dismissed it with a wave of the hand. "I hadn't even noticed you were being short with me. I'm sorry you're distracted. Is there anything we can do to help?"

"See." He pointed at Allegra. "The rest of you jump up my behind, giving me grief, but sweet Allegra here asks how she can help."

"Oh, poor widdle Tomasso," Valentina said. "Can I get you a diaper and a bottle of warm milk?" She smiled at Lorenzo, who pretended he was sucking on a pacifier.

"You two best stop or I'll make you sit in a corner like I did when you were children, with your noses touching." Fabiana's lips formed a thin line.

Valentina faked a look of horror on her face. "Anything but that! With Tomasso? I'd have to smell his breath up close and everything? I promise, I'll repent!" She stuck her tongue out at her brother.

"So, Tomasso, what can we do to help you?" His mother reached for the marmalade for her cornetto. "You must be anxious about your upcoming departure to New York."

He shrugged. He had been so preoccupied with thoughts of Gisele even his dream job was taking a second seat to it.

"How about finding me a place to stay?"

Valentina wrinkled her brow. "You're moving to New York for several months and still you haven't found a place to live?"

He held his hands up. "So shoot me." He frowned. "I've been preoccupied with other things. I hadn't gotten around to it yet. I was hoping I could find some family in New York, but so far nothing has materialized."

Valentina leaned against the table, one arm draped over the edge, her other elbow resting on it, her hand on her chin. "You need a place to stay in New York City, eh?" She

scratched her chin in thought.

"Yeah. You've got an apartment for me?"

"Maybe something better," she said. "Perhaps you can make your little sister happy while she provides you a perfect place to stay while you're in New York."

He cocked his brow. "You're a real estate broker now, are you?"

"Much better than that," she said. "I'm a lonely woman wanting to figure out how to get the man in my life to stay for an extended visit. And you, my favorite brother—"

Lorenzo smirked at her. "I thought that was me."

She shook her head. "Not this time." She curled her finger toward Tomasso, beckoning him. "You, my favorite brother, are about to make my life that much easier."

Chapter Eight

"**I'VE** got great news!" Parker said as he stood at the stove, scrambling some eggs. "I'm going to Italy!"

Gisele's eyes opened wide. "Like, taking off a week of work to visit Valentina?"

He shook his head. "Even better," he said. "I'm going to take a few months off, kind of like a sabbatical, to spend some time with Valentina in Chianti, see how we really get along, if we have the makings of a long-term thing or not."

"Wow." Gisele frowned. "So just like that"—she snapped her fingers for emphasis—"you're leaving me?"

He held up his hands to assure her. "It's not 'like that.'" He ground some pepper into the eggs and took a small taste. "I'm not leaving you, per se. More like I'm taking a little extended vacation."

"But that means you'll be there, and I'll be here." She pursed her lips. The two of them had been together nonstop, basically, since their mother died. She knew, intellectually, that someday Parker would have to claim his own life again, but in practice, the idea seemed a bit heartbreaking.

"I'm sorry, G." Parker turned off the stove and scooped eggs onto her plate, then his. "It's nothing personal. But I've been kind of burning out on work anyhow. And while I know it seems sudden, now that we're apart, I miss Valentina and I'd like to spend some more time with her."

"Why doesn't she just come here then?" Gisele grabbed ketchup from the fridge and sat at the breakfast table.

"It's not that easy. She has a fledgling business to deal with and a lot of family commitments."

Gisele scowled as she made a ketchup puddle on her plate and began distractedly swirling her egg in it. "But you've got family commitments too, you know."

He cocked an eyebrow as he spread butter on his toast. "I do?"

"Um, yeah you do. Like as in me. Your only sister. Make that only remaining relative. Or are you prepared to simply dump me like Dad did?"

"Hey"—he reached over to put a hand on her shoulder—"you know I'm not 'dumping' you. I'm not leaving you, sweetie. You'll always be my sister and our lives will always be intermingled. But I am approaching my thirties, and it's high time I did something about my own personal life at this point. Don't you think so?"

She sighed. "I guess. But I'd like to go on record saying I don't like it. Not one bit. What am I going to do without you?"

Her brother patted her on her head. "Maybe you can go to work every day like you've been doing for years now. And you can get together with friends, and hey, maybe while I'm gone you'll meet a nice young man."

She rolled her eyes. "Trust me, *that's* not gonna happen."

"Why not?" he said. "It would be good for you to put

yourself out there."

"Oh, so I can think I've fallen in love and go through all the hoops of fire and have a big stupid wedding only to find I'm stuck with some jerk who starts to resent me and I don't even realize he's sleeping around on me and then I have babies and he leaves and never comes back? Thanks, but no thanks."

Parker took a bite of his eggs. "You do know that all men aren't like our father, don't you?"

"Well, you're not. But even you won't stick around. Leaving me alone in the cold, cruel city while you gallivant across the Tuscan countryside."

"If you're trying to make me feel guilty, you're doing a bang-up job."

Gisele looked up at her brother and wrinkled her forehead. "I'm sorry. That's not fair of me, I know. It's only that I'm going to miss you in a bad way. Because it's always been you and me, and now it's just going to be me." A tear formed in the corner of her eyes.

Parker pushed back from the table and stood up, reaching a hand out for his little sister. "Come here, you." He pulled her toward him and dabbed at her tears with his sleeve. "I guess it wasn't fair of me to up and leave you all alone, no warning, was it? Hard enough to have your beloved brother not here." He winked and she smiled through her tears. "But to do that and leave you to rattle around this place all on your own... that wasn't very thoughtful of me, was it?"

She thrust out her lower lip in a pout. "It's okay." She sniffled. "I totally get that you need to live your life. I don't want to hold you back. That would be obnoxious of me anyhow."

He scruffed her hair, then tucked a strand of it behind her ear. "Nothing you could do would ever be obnoxious, G. You're the best kid sister a guy could ever have. We'll figure this out. Trust me, I'll make sure you're in good hands."

"Sooo…" Valentina said as she opened a bottle of Brunello from one of the family's vineyards located in Montalcino, to the south of Chianti. She poured a small amount into her glass, then swirled it before taking a sip, letting it roll off her tongue as she breathed it in. She smiled as she swallowed it. "That always makes my day. Anyhow, back to our discussion." She turned to Tomasso, who was on his phone, totally ignoring her.

"Hello, Tomasso!"

She tapped him on the shoulder and handed him a glass of wine. Finally he looked up and shook his head to escape the fog he was in.

"Sorry, *cara*," he said. "Busy talking reclaimed wood on Facebook."

She arched her eyebrows. "Boy, you sure know how to have a good time, don't you?"

"Stop, Valentina." He repeated what his sister had just done with her wine before swallowing a sip. "It's what makes my day. It's my passion."

She scratched his head affectionately before sitting down next to him. "I know. It's why I don't tease you too much about it. Plus you're scary talented. I don't want you to disown me when you're rich and famous because I mocked for being a woodworking geek."

"Newsflash: we're already rich and famous."

She held up her glass to the light, momentarily lost in thought. "Huh. I guess you've got a point there. Though the Romeo fame isn't quite the same. I mean it has little to do with us and everything to do with our ancestors. Whereas your fame will have everything to do with your skills."

Tomasso chuckled. "Yeah, well, I don't think you need to worry about my leaving you in the dust anytime soon. I've yet to hear of any wood-carvers whose names are on the tip of your average tongue."

"Paul Bunyan?"

He laughed. "I think he was a lumberjack. And he wasn't even real. But nice try."

"So you excited for this new adventure?"

His eyes lit up. "Are you kidding? This is my dream come true. I'll be working with the world-famous Grady O'Malley, who's spent his whole career restoring the woodworking in historic brownstones in Manhattan from the golden age of New York City."

One of their kitties, a calico named Gatto—Italian, for cat—jumped into Valentina's lap. "Hmm… world-famous Grady O'Malley, but I've never heard of him. I guess that's in keeping with that notion that no wood-carver's name is on the tip of your average tongue."

"You've proven your point there, although you even met the man when he was here." She shrugged, clearly unimpressed with the magnitude of the man's talent.

"So Mamma tells me you're still trying to find a

temporary place to stay."

"I've got a bead on a few places, but so far nothing much has materialized."

"Perfect. Because I've got the answer to your prayers."

Tomasso took a sip of wine. "Do tell."

"Here's the deal. Parker is coming to spend a few months here. We'd like to see if we can make a go of it in the same place at the same time for a while without killing each other, maybe see how compatible we are. Which means his place is empty and you can stay there!"

Tomasso's eyes widened. "Seriously? No strings attached, I just get to hold down the fort at his house?"

"It's all yours. You won't even have to feed a cat or walk a dog. Simply show up. I already have the passcode for you to get into the house, and you'll be good to go."

"Valentina! I always said you were my favorite sister. And now you've proven it once again. Don't forget to remind Lorenzo that you went out of your way to do your favorite brother a solid. Thanks!"

"You're most welcome. I think you'll have a great time. From what I hear it's an amazing home—I believe it's one of those historic brownstones like you were talking about. Plus, Parker said it had been, quote, 'lovingly restored' about eight years ago."

"Damn, this makes things super easy for me. And he's in the city? Not like an hour away in the suburbs?"

"He said it was on the Upper West Side. A beautiful tree-lined street."

Tomasso gave his sister a huge hug. "I can't thank you enough. This will be the best three months of my life."

Chapter Nine

"SO I gave our conversation the other day a lot of thought," Parker said as he packed two large suitcases for the next three months. Gisele was sad that he would be gone in a matter of days, leaving her alone to feel like the only person on the entire island of Manhattan. She was good at self-pity, she knew.

"Does this mean you've changed your mind and you're only going for a few days then you'll be back?" She gave him a big, fake, wishful, toothy grin while batting her eyelashes to lay it on thick.

He shook his head and scruffed her hair. "No such luck. But I did have a stroke of genius that you're going to love. Well, to be truthful, Valentina had the brilliant idea."

Gisele lifted an eyebrow. "She's going to send a surrogate in your stead?"

Parker clapped. "Brava! How'd you figure that out?"

Her eyebrows pressed downward. "Wait—what do you mean? I was just joking."

"In that case, I have a wonderful surprise for you. You see, I wasn't comfortable with the idea of you being in this big old house all by yourself. Besides, I hate to up and abandon you. So I've found the perfect houseguest to keep you company while I'm out of the country. I think you two will have a fantastic time. I mean he told me when we were in Monaforte that you'd both had some in-depth conversations leading up to the wedding, so I'm comfortable that you've at least gotten to know each other. In other words, it's not like I'm dropping a complete stranger in your lap. And I get to feel good about you having someone who's got your back. Plus you've got some great company."

Gisele's heartbeat started racing and her breathing became shallow. For a minute, she thought she might hyperventilate. Either that or blow an aneurysm. "Oh, my God. Please, whatever you do, do not tell me what I think you're about to tell me."

"What?"

"You're not planning on sending that brother of hers to stay here, are you?"

"Wow. Good guess! Your spidey sense was spot-on with that one. Turns out Tomasso has to be in Manhattan for a few months for an apprenticeship and Valentina told me he was having a hard time finding a short-term lease. He's going to move into our place while I'm gone. That way you're not alone, and you're much safer with a strong man in the house."

Gisele tried to object but the words seemed frozen in her throat. "But—"

"Isn't it great?"

At last she was able to get the words out of her mouth. "It's not great at all. I do not want that asshole in my house and I veto it. You should have asked me first. He's a first-class, grade-A jerk, and he can go live under a bridge span in a cardboard box as far as I'm concerned. Because he's not living here with me."

Parker furrowed his brows. "But G.—you were all sad at being alone in the city."

"Please, Parker. Seriously? Alone in the city? Isn't that an oxymoron? By the very nature of it being a city, I'm not alone. I'll be keeping company with one-and-a-half million other folks here on this island, and I will not be even remotely alone. You can go ahead and call him and cancel that."

Parker shook his head. "Sorry, Gisele. It's simply not possible. I've offered the place up to him and he's gladly accepted. Look, he's Valentina's brother, he's a good guy, and he needs a place to stay. It would be rude of me not to have offered it to him, and now that I have, it's a done deal. Besides, I don't want you alone in this big old house. I want to feel safe knowing you're safe. This matter is closed."

"Parker that's not fair! You can't do that to me. He's the worst."

"I know for a fact that Tomasso is a good man who comes from a good family. His sister would never have suggested he move in here if she wasn't certain he would be the ultimate gentleman. Whatever issue you have with him, I'll ask you to keep it to yourself and be the best hostess you can to our houseguest. He, in turn, will be a respectful and helpful guest and everyone will have a wonderful time."

Gisele growled. "I'll tell you who will be having a good time: you and Valentina. You'll be sexing your way through Italy while I'm here having shouting matches with the rudest, most ignorant, ugliest, meanest man I've ever met from Italy."

Her brother grinned. "Well, considering he's likely the only man you've met from Italy, that's not saying much." He patted her on the back. "I trust you're exaggerating

matters a bit. I'm sure you can work out whatever your differences are."

Gisele stuck out her tongue. "And I trust I won't speak to you for the next three months either. Good-bye."

She turned and left his room, slamming the door behind her.

This was going to suck massively. Imprisoned in her own house with the Hunchback of Romeo Wines. More like the troll from beneath the bridge in the "Three Billy Goats Gruff." Ugh.

Chapter Ten

IT was approaching midnight by the time Tomasso finally settled in for the taxi ride from JFK Airport, thanks to flight delays, an interminable wait at customs, and a ridiculously long taxi line. When he arrived at Parker's place, he was totally beat and ready for bed. As the cabbie pulled up, he sized up the brownstone, extremely impressed. It was a beautiful Italianate building, with tall windows and a stone stoop flanked by gorgeous, heavy cast iron railings and elaborately decorated newel posts and balusters. The majestic-looking doorway was flanked by large columns with ornate capitals that supported heavy door hoods, a dramatic carved keystone above the door, and acanthus brackets on either side. He looked up to notice the generous mansard roof and wondered if beneath that roofline was an artist's garret: how he'd love to have a workspace like that overlooking views of the city. He also wondered why a single guy would live alone in such a huge place. *Must be even more loaded than I thought.* Oh well, at least he wasn't after Valentina's money.

A heavy snow began to fall as the cabbie helped him unload his bags while Tomasso rifled around for his phone so he could pull up the passcode to get into the place. After mounting the steps, he punched in the key code and pushed

open the large mahogany-and-beveled-glass door, desperate for sleep. His ears were killing him from the pressure change and he felt a cold coming on. At least he wouldn't have to deal with anyone for a day or two while he adjusted to the time change and caught up on sleep. All Tomasso wanted was to be left alone.

He didn't even bother to turn on the lights when he got inside. Exhausted, he opted not to explore the place—he'd save that for daylight. Parker told him he could occupy the master suite at the very top of the first flight of steps, and with a suitcase in each hand and a laptop bag slung over his shoulders, he trudged up the steps and entered the bedroom that would be his for the next few months.

He was too tired to even bother brushing his teeth. Instead he stripped down to his boxer briefs, tossing his clothes on a nearby chair, buried himself beneath the covers, and promptly passed out. For all of about four hours, curse that jetlag. He felt as if he'd barely slept a wink before he was wide awake, staring at the ceiling, yearning to drift back into a state of stupor. He tried to persuade his brain that he was indeed tired, to no avail. After tossing and turning for an hour, he finally he got up, splashed some cold water on his face, gave his teeth a good scrubbing, and decided to explore the place. He tucked his laptop beneath his arm as he opened his bedroom door, only to crash into something, or someone, causing him to scream out loud.

Gisele's alarm went off earlier than usual. She had to be in the studio by seven for a celebrity interview her boss was producing. With last night's snow, she knew it would take even longer to actually get to the office, so she'd set the alarm for forty-five minutes early. These dark, wintry days made it that much harder to wake up. With Parker gone and no one to share breakfast with, she was tired and cranky and alone, even though he'd only left a day ago.

She wasn't sure when the Royal Jerk—ha-ha, he was part royalty, and that did make him a royal sort of jerk, didn't it?—was supposed to arrive. At least Parker would give her advance notice prior to Tomasso's arrival, she figured. So she could leave town. Or barricade the door shut. Or put fire ants in his bed.

Until then, it would be only her, besides the occasional visit from their housekeeper Rosa, who'd been with the Hornsby family since Gisele was a small child. Thank goodness for Rosa—while she could never replace her own mom, she was practically a second mother to Gisele and Parker, and Gisele would be especially grateful for Rosa's presence now that Parker had flown the coop.

She'd scrambled to get ready, throwing on a pair of black jeans and gray cashmere cable-knit sweater. She grabbed a scarf and draped it around her neck, rearranging it six times until it finally looked right. What was it about those damned scarves? You could never make them look normal the way they always looked in fashion magazines. She blamed the Italians, who were so effortlessly fashionable they made everyone else look bad.

Of course, she blamed the Italians because of the only Italian she actively loathed. The whole damned country would have to take the heat because of him. Gisele swiped on her favorite pinkish-nude lip gloss, slipped on a pair of grungy cowboy boots that she didn't mind mucking up in the snow, grabbed her purse, and flicked off her bedroom light before stepping out into the hallway. She hated even walking past Parker's room, what with it empty now. At least until the Royal Pain arrived, at which point she'd have to figure out how to get downstairs without passing by that bedroom door. Perhaps she could jump out her bedroom window.

"Ugh," she said out loud, lost in thought, dreading his arrival, right as she crashed head-on into a tall, warm, nearly naked body in front of that very door.

"Ack!" she said as she threw her purse down and lifted her arms up, ready to hit whoever it was. As if that was going to help with a naked intruder.

"Gah!" said a man's voice as the body attached to it pushed back against her after her sticky lips collided with his chest.

Gisele's heart raced. Holy shit. There was a stranger in her house and she didn't even know what to do. Maybe Parker was right about her needing protection from intruders. Even if it meant having that Rotten Romeo guy living under the roof. But too late—here was this person, and he wasn't even dressed, and she didn't even have the putative protection of the Toad from Tuscany yet.

She didn't know quite what to do, so on impulse, she screamed, karate chopped the man across the chest, then grabbed his forearm and bit down hard.

"Ouch! Goddammit!" He flicked on a nearby switch, bathing the scene in light, then stood, staring at the culprit. "What the hell? Gisele? What are you doing in your brother's house?"

"My *brother's* house?" she said as she spat his arm out of her mouth, wiping her tongue on her sleeve as if she'd had contact with the cooties. "This is my place, buster. And what are you doing here? You didn't even have the decency to let me know when you'd be showing up? Instead you decide to scare the crap out of me in the middle of the night?"

Tomasso shook his arm, attempting to mitigate the pain from what she figured was the now-throbbing bite on his forearm. Served him right. "Crap, you've got sharp teeth. Are you a vampire on the side or something?"

She glared at him. "You'd be lucky if I was." She circled him like a predator finishing off the kill. "At least then I'd put you out of your misery. Or I'd be done being miserable once I killed you. Not that I'm miserable, mind you. And not that I want to kill you, for that matter. It's simply that, well, listen up, buddy. This is my place." She poked her finger into his chest. "You got that?"

He held up his hands, surrendering.

"And you're going to do as I say. Understand?" She took a deep breath, collecting herself from the scare. "I had no choice in the matter with you coming to live here, but I'm going to make damn good and sure you do things on my terms now that you're here." She stood with her hands on her hips in a Wonder Woman power pose. She'd read somewhere that by standing as if you're strong and fierce, you adopt those characteristics. "Starting with no more near-nakedness. None. If you want to be nude, then go to your room and shut the door. But around me, you must be fully clothed. At all times."

Her first rule, made up on the spot, had more to do with the fact that she might weaken her resolve if she had to look at his sexy chest and those slim hips and the bulge in his boxers. Then she'd remember what it felt like being up close and personal with that very protuberance. But she was so not going there. He could keep his hot body to himself, thank you.

"Rule number two." She held up her pointer finger and middle finger for emphasis. "Pretend I'm not here at all times."

Tomasso raised his hands.

She shook her head. "Save your questions until the end."

"The end of time? Or the end of your diatribe?"

"Ha-ha. This isn't a diatribe. I'm laying down the ground rules for your intrusion on my privacy."

"But this is important," he said, rubbing his hand along his abdomen in that way that guys do that makes girls crazy because they'd rather have their hands doing that instead.

She nodded, her lips pursed. "Fine, but keep it quick."

"So if I'm to pretend you're not here, then why can't I wander around half-naked? I mean, if you're not here, the fact is, I like to be comfortable, and sometimes that means wearing only my underwear, or even nothing at—"

Gisele groaned. "Whatever. Just don't be naked near me. That is punishable by immediate expulsion from the premises. Which means you'll be sleeping on a park bench in Central Park. And you'll freeze to death. Except that they'll arrest you first. Which means maybe you'll end up on Riker's Island. Which won't be pleasant. You can be naked there all you want. But you'll last about a minute."

"You're all heart." Tomasso shook his head.

"Takes one to know one." She almost couldn't believe she'd invoked that childish taunt, but there you had it:

Gisele Hornsby had officially been reduced to toddler status by the presence of this vexing man.

"For the record, I was entirely unaware I was intruding on your privacy."

"Sure. You didn't know I'd be here." She crossed her arms and wrinkled her brow.

"I hadn't a clue. As far as I knew, I would be living alone here. Last night, I got in late and went to bed. I couldn't sleep. I woke up. And now I have the Archangel of Hades biting my arm—breaking skin, no less—and karate chopping me for no good reason."

"Well, what was I supposed to do?"

"Hell if I know. All I can tell you is my sister said Parker was going to visit her for a while and his place was empty. I was coming here for a wood carving apprenticeship and I hadn't had any luck finding a temporary place to stay. Your brother offered for me to stay here."

"And no one bothered to mention to you that Parker and I live together in our parents' house?"

"I don't even know who your parents are, so no. I hadn't a clue."

She glared at him. "My parents are to be left out of this."

He glared back and screwed his finger by his temple, indicating he thought she was crazy. "You're the one who brought up your parents. I didn't!"

Gisele glanced at her watch. "Look, I have to get to work or I'll get fired. Stay out of my room, don't touch anything you shouldn't touch, and leave me the hell alone." She grabbed her purse and turned on her heel. "And have a nice day." She stomped loudly down the steps.

Jenny Gardiner

A minute later she threw her big down jacket on and pulled a hat over her head against the elements, slamming the door behind her for emphasis.

She knew it was going to be a crap day and it had just gotten much, much worse.

Chapter Eleven

"WELL, shoot," Gisele muttered as she slipped along the street approaching her office, almost landing on her butt. *All I wanted was a nice warm muffin and a hot cup of coffee and now I'm starting my day instead with a cold blast of like-it-or-not. Not to mention what was likely a particularly warm bun attached to that Wretched Romeo.* The last thing she could let herself think about was what his buns felt like in her hands, so she banished that thought to the no-man's land section of her brain, along with all other foolish initial impressions of Tomasso Romeo that turned out to be completely wrong. *What a bummer.*

Gisele tried to divert to a coffee shop in the lobby of her building, but the line was twenty deep and there was no way she could make it by seven if she attempted that. Her stomach growled and her brain silently did as well. She lined up with the masses to catch the next elevator and mercifully wedged herself in right as the doors began to close on the first available lift. For the entire thirty-eight floors up, she stood stiff like a soldier, arms pressed to her body, and packed in to tightly she could barely breathe.

The elevator opened and belched her and several others out into her office. As she shook out her limbs, she could hear her boss, Sophie Pellegrino shouting in the next room.

"Let's go, people, we don't have all day," she said, clapping her hands. Gisele peeled off her coat and looked at the clock on the wall: five minutes after seven. Of course it was.

"You're late," Sophie said as Gisele turned the corner. "What part of 'be on time' did you not understand?"

Gisele rolled her eyes. It helped that her boss was one of her best friends. "I'm sorry, Soph," she said. "It's been one of those days." She shook her head. "Actually, it's been way worse than one of those days. It's been a shit sandwich kind of day and I've barely taken a bite of the thing before spitting it out, so I'm not holding my breath for the rest of the day to get much better."

Sophie crossed her arms and lifted her brow. "I can't begin to imagine what has happened to make you, my cheerful, perennial glass-half-full production assistant, show up sounding so miserable. Did a clown arrive on your doorstep, threatening to abduct you?"

"Worse, if you can imagine. And I have a deathly fear of clowns."

Sophie tapped her fingernail on her arm. "Do tell."

"So you remember I told you about the Italian Stallion, right?"

Sophie nodded. "The man who was packing—"

"Shhh!" Gisele held her finger up to her lips. "Not like I want to advertise this to the whole office."

"So he had a big dick! That's a good thing. You should shout that to the world."

"Stop! Besides, I know nothing about the size of his—" Gisele crossed her fingers behind her back because, well, she didn't want to get struck down by lightning for that little white lie.

"Ladies! Would love to hear you discuss my manhood in greater detail, but time's a-wastin'!" Justin Magruder, the assistant producer and their veritable third musketeer said as he draped his arms over their shoulders in a huddle.

"Yes, but I'm the boss and I call the shots around here," Sophie said. "And Gisele was just telling me about her man with the humongous—" she held up her hands, allowing a good foot of air space to linger between her palms, and smiled broadly.

"Oh, my God. I am never going to confide in you if you're gonna broadcast this to the universe!"

Sophie winked at Justin conspiratorially. "Being that our dear friend Justin far prefers men to women, I'm sure he'd be more than happy to hear about what your man is packing as well. Right, Justin?"

"I promise I won't judge. Pinky swear." He hooked his little finger and extended it to Gisele.

Gisele shrieked but in a joking way. "All right, fine, you two. But stop interrupting me or we'll be here till lunchtime and I'm already starved and we have a show to tape. Besides, he is unequivocally *not* my man."

"Sorry—didn't I tell you? The interview's been postponed till this afternoon. I was only giving you grief for being late when you got here. We can talk all morning."

"More importantly this means I can go eat something now."

"If only that Italian Stallion of yours was around, you could have *him* for breakfast."

Gisele groaned. "That's the thing. He *is* around."

"Wait—he's here? The man your brother was forcing on you like some poor goose about to become foie gras?"

Gisele nodded. "One and the same. Only I didn't even get a warning. He showed up after I went to bed last night. I ran into him—quite literally—as I was trying to get out the door this morning."

"Ran into him, eh?" Sophie steepled her fingers and drummed them together as she looked at Justin, her eyebrow lifted.

"He was standing in the dark in the hallway outside my brother's room and practically naked."

"Now you're speaking my language." Justin pulled up a chair and sat down, crossing his legs and leaning in, his warm brown eyes fixed on Gisele. Sophie dragged another one over and parked herself in it. "Like, how naked?" he said.

"Well, I mean, it was dark, and it's not like I was feeling around for the full monty. But his chest was bare and his legs were bare and, well, when he finally turned the light on, he had on a pair of that clingy underwear, like they're boxers but they aren't loose."

"The make-no-mistake-about-it kind." Justin clutched his hand and pulled back his elbow, a victory cheer. "Yes! I like this guy already." He scraped his fingers through his dirty blond hair.

Sophie burst out laughing. "I prefer those too. You know what you're dealing with right off the bat." She laughed again. "Bat, get it? Like a big baseball bat? Oh, imagine if he was hung like a baseball bat."

Sophie shook her head. "I'm so glad my friends can laugh at my expense."

"All right, so then what? You were late because he scooped you into his arms and pulled you into the bedroom and dropped you on the bed and you made mad passionate love—"

"Eww, on my brother's bed? Yuck. No thanks. Plus that would have been for all of one-and-a-half seconds, to avoid being late for work. No, you doof. I read him the riot act."

"What?" Justin leaned his elbow on his knee while he kicked his leg back and forth impatiently. "Why would you do that with a sexy naked man with a huge boner?"

"He wasn't naked and when did I ever say anything about his erection?"

"Remember, you told me all about that after you got back from that wedding," Sophie said, waving her hand dismissively.

"Aha! So he has a big one then. This is all good news, Gisele."

"No, it is not! Even if he has a boner that acts like a perpetually springing fountain, it is not okay. The man dissed me not once but twice. Make that three times. Oh, hell, I've lost count. He was happy to take advantage of me but then he humiliated me and that is not the type of man I want half-naked in my hallway at five in the morning."

"That's the type of man I want completely naked in my *bed* at five in the morning. Trust me, pride is overrated." Justin high-fived Sophie as the two of them laughed.

"So when you read him the riot act, what exactly did that mean?" Sophie leaned in to hear the details.

"I told him no more naked stuff. And to leave me alone. And to pretend I wasn't there."

Sophie crossed her hands over her heart and fluttered her eyelashes, mocking her friend. "Such a romantic, our girl Gisele is, isn't she, Justin?"

"Charm school graduate, she is."

"You two are being insufferable. What was I supposed to do? My brother forces this guy on me to 'protect' me." She made air quotes as she snarled her lip. "And now I'm stuck with this guy who—"

"With whom you'd love to finish what you started?" Sophie looked at her long and hard.

Gisele scrunched her nose as if she smelled a rotten egg. "Does that make me pathetic if I admit that I'm still attracted to him even though he was a jerk to me?"

"It makes you human, sweetie." Sophie rubbed her friend's shoulder. "From the sounds of it, you had a great time until he got cold feet. Maybe his cold feet had nothing to do with you and everything to do with him. Did you ever think about that?"

She shrugged. "I shouldn't have to think about that. I mean I am not into playing stupid games. I'm honest with people and I expect them to be honest with me too."

"I get that. And in an ideal world, that's how the battle between the sexes would play out—in the bedroom, and everybody wins. But people are odd ducks sometimes. And occasionally it takes a bit of detective work to figure out if what they say is even what they mean. My guess is, given the state of his, er, state when you got down and dirty with him in Monaforte, he had it bad for you. If he didn't, it's not like you'd have had a chance to play with his ever-so-glorious cock. Am I right?" This time it was Sophie's turn to fist-bump Justin after her little mother-daughteresque speech. Not that any real mom would actually speak so candidly to her girl, but still.

Gisele paced back and forth, shaking her head. "I'm not even going there. Once burned, twice shy. Twice burned, shame on me."

"To mix a couple of overheated metaphors," Justin said.

"See, I've been driven to clichés by this man. It's that bad."

"So why don't you let things unfold organically, see where they lead."

Justin slapped Sophie on the back playfully. "I thought you were going to say unfold orgasmically. Which is what I'd vote for."

"That's what I'd do because I like to have fun, but obviously Gisele is a little more tentative about this than you or me."

"So barring unforeseen orgasms, why don't you chill out a little bit, give the guy some space, maybe even consider pressing the reset button, and let things go. The good news is you live in a big house. Technically you could avoid him."

"Yeah, if I schedule my meals when he's not there or hide out in my bedroom instead of watching television in the living room like I normally would."

"Now, if you want to accelerate things, you could put on a sexy little French maid costume and in no time flat, you'll have him eating out of your—"

Gisele held up her hand. "Enough. No more visuals from you two. I'm going to have to grit my teeth and bare it for the next couple of months."

"And think of England," Justin said, referring to the supposed advice mothers would give their daughters for their wedding night.

Sophie stood up and waggled her finger. "Au contraire, my friend. I would think fondly of Monaforte." She winked at Gisele as she left her friend to ponder that memory.

Chapter Twelve

THINGS had gotten off to such a rollicking start for poor Tomasso. He was more than happy to be alone at home during the day while his adversary toiled in the salt mines or wherever she was employed. She certainly wasn't working in the sugar mills, because there wasn't a hint of sweetness to her any longer. How frustrating—his attempts at honesty merely came across as nothing more than an enormous insult to her. But who was he to understand a woman's mind?

He'd finally started working with Grady O'Malley and was focused on fine-tuning his woodcarving skills. From the minute he stepped foot inside the man's legendary warehouse in Brooklyn, he was completely mesmerized. Grady was an artistic genius, and his vast warehouse was filled to capacity with life-size woodcarvings and all sorts of works in progress he was creating for stately homes throughout the region: doorways, scrolls, wood panels, railings, balustrades, and statues.

Grady had been one of the many artisans recruited to help make the Romeo wines corporate headquarters the most talked about building in Italy. It was there that Grady and Tomasso hit it off. The artisan had offered to mentor Tomasso, who had taken a great interest in antique figureheads—the large wooden figures that jutted out of the prow of old sailing ships.

While working on any number of relief carvings—wooden carvings that appear to rise out of the wood as if they are coming alive—Tomasso hoped to create his very own figurehead. Indeed he had no sailing vessel on which to place it, but that was irrelevant. It was about the journey. He didn't even know yet what he would carve. He was leaning toward a mermaid, but perhaps a sea nymph or some siren might call to him as well.

Each day, Tomasso set about practicing his craft, starting with a long piece of Brazilian mahogany and a V-shaped gouge chisel to first carve his outline. Grady had him work on a floral panel that would be used in the library of a patron who was paying big money for fine work, which meant that Grady had complete faith that Tomasso could execute his carvings superbly. The work required intense concentration—a relief for Tomasso. It took his mind off the line-in-the-sand battleground that staying in Parker's house had become. In fact, last night, Gisele quite literally took a piece of chalk and drew a demarcation down the center of the kitchen floor.

"You stay on that side, and I stay on this side," she said as she prepared to make dinner. It figured her side had the refrigerator and the cooktop as well as the sink, giving her a distinct advantage. Which, of course, was too bad for her, because Tomasso was a fabulous cook and would have happily shared his meals with her, had he been able to whip something up with ease rather than relegated to meal delivery.

This meant Tomasso would have to wait until Gisele was done in the kitchen for the night, and then he'd cook himself some dinner, crossing her damned chalk line with glee. And that was fine: he was European and used to dining late. It didn't matter to him philosophically; rather it was just unfortunate to have this undeclared standoff festering between the two of them.

But he wasn't going to think about that. Nor was he going to think about that hair of hers, which she'd worn falling off her shoulders in soft curls last night. The very way he'd remembered it as he looked down at her when she swiped her soft, pink tongue across the tip of his hardened shaft. But he wasn't going to think about that either, or how perfectly those yoga pants hugged her ass. Nor how he could see the outline of her nipples, clear as day when she wore only the jog bra with the yoga pants while cooking dinner, claiming she was overheated. He wanted badly to show her what overheated meant. But he wasn't going to think about that. He closed his eyes for a minute to try to eradicate all thoughts of the woman from his mind and returned to his craft.

He was acutely aware that each press of the gouge chisel pushed against delicate wood fibers, which ran the danger of splitting the wood and ruining the project, so he reminded himself constantly to cut in the opposite direction of the wood grain. Not that the press of the gouge brought to mind what it would be like to press into her body. That was nothing he would consider while taking such care not to ruin this expensive piece of wood entrusted to him.

Each time he got to the apex of a curve, he had to reverse the cut again, always making sure all wood fibers were being supported. And not even once did thinking about a curve bring to mind the crest of her breast, the hardened tip of that nipple as he wrapped his lips around it.

Because thinking about that would be professional suicide right now.

He cut a trench around each new section of design to help reinforce the support. With each stop cut he made, he'd start digging out the background, creating the "relief" that made it appear as if the figures were rising from the wood. It was its own sort of magic. Maybe not the same type of magic that came with the merging of his body with hers, something he deeply regretted never having achieved when he had the chance. Because he couldn't get that notion out of his head, and it made him hard just thinking about it.

"Remember to visualize your design in three dimensions," Grady said. "Understand what it will look like, that you will have figures layered on top or beneath each other, and plan accordingly. That means stepping down the image, one part at a time. Define the edges of a layer by making downward stop cuts around it, then lower the layer next to it. Creating realistic images is all about knowing what to lower and where to lower it." Tomasso pondered that concept of figures on top or beneath each other: him lying on his back, Gisele on top, riding his hard cock, her breasts moving with the wild sexual thrash of her body. Jesus, he was going to need hypnosis to clear his mind of that woman.

Tomasso had actually had plenty of practice carving alongside Grady back home, but here he was refining his skills and committing it to such muscle memory that he hoped to be more fail-safe. Nothing worse than being halfway through carving a piece of wood only to have it split and ruined. Or halfway to climax with a beautiful woman's mouth on your cock when you're cut off.

Finally legitimizing his gift helped Tomasso feel a kinship to his heritage. Throughout history, Italy was full of gifted artisans who sculpted in a variety of media, creating masterpieces that survive to this day. Not that he would ever be as great as Michelangelo, but he had a talent that he was finally able to nurture, and it pleased him to no end. If only he could exorcise that woman from his mind to clear away needless distractions.

It was usually past dark when Tomasso finally left the warehouse and returned to the brownstone. One night he arrived home well after eight to an empty house. Which was a little bit sad, especially since he was accustomed back home to being in a large household filled with robust activity at all hours. At least it was preferable to Gisele's palpable silence that had greeted him the past week or so.

As he mounted the steps, he called out her name but there was no response, so he went into his room and took a quick shower to get the wood dust off of him. Only then did he remember he was out of clean underwear. Wrapping a towel around his hips, he went down the hall to the laundry room, where he'd left a load of clothes in the dryer. He noticed Gisele's door was wide open, and her light was on. He poked his head in, only to find it empty. He'd never seen the inside of her room before and wondered if it would be void of mirrors—didn't those things kill vampires?

Standing in the doorway, he peered into what seemed a perfectly normal-looking girl's bedroom. No human sacrifices lying around, no bubbling cauldron of eye of newt, nothing strange at all. To his left was a large bed with a bright orange and hot pink floral duvet, and at the head of it were about a thousand oversized pillows. He figured it would take her an hour to toss all those pillows down before she could even get into bed at night. Or if it were up to him, he'd toss her on top of them, to hell with moving them out of the way. A pillow beneath her lower back would give him much easier access anyway… Gah! He had to get that notion out of his head (make that both heads). It would only torment him.

Despite himself and with great trepidation, he slowly entered the dead zone. Something about Gisele called to him in here. He had no clue what it was, but in this room, he sensed he could find the cure to whatever it was that ailed him or her or them. At least it might enable them to be friends while he lived here. At this point, that would have to be good enough. He was sick and tired of being tangled up in her anger trap.

A bulletin board framed in white wicker hung on the wall to his right. Pinned to it were a couple of certificates: Varsity Club, Honor Roll, and several newspaper articles. He looked around again, making certain no one was around, and tiptoed toward it for a closer look.

Marilyn Franklin Hornsby, he read aloud from a faded newspaper clipping of an obituary as he ran his fingers along the printed words. He read more about her: beloved mother of Gisele Annabelle and Parker Hampton. He did the math on the year of her birth to the year of her death: she was only forty-three years old. He tried to read on to discover how she died, but there was no reference to cause of death. Nor was there mention of a husband, which was curious.

Marilyn Hornsby came from some money, it seemed. The list of previously deceased relatives sounded long and illustrious, based on references to her parents and grandparents, all of whom were patrons of the arts in Manhattan, and after whom, it seemed, a few buildings had been named.

Tomasso looked on the desk below, where pictures mostly of Gisele and Parker stood—at least he assumed it was them at much earlier ages. In one, they were on a ride at an amusement park; Gisele's face looked a little peaked like she was about to be sick, while her brother beamed. She looked around eight or so. In another, the two of them were sitting on a beach, drinking cans of Coke as they worked on a sand castle. Gisele appeared to be in the first blush of puberty, her small but visible breasts covered by a floral bikini. There were pictures of them as they got older, one with Parker in graduation cap and gown as they stood alongside their mother, who was the mirror image of Gisele. But Tomasso was still trying to find any sign of a father. Finally, pinned on the bulletin board behind the obituary was the sole reference to Edward Parker Hornsby: a wedding announcement that showed a picture of a man, who shared many of Parker's features, with a much younger woman, who looked nothing like Gisele's mother.

So her father was one of those. Which would explain Gisele's irritation at what she would see as Tomasso's cavalier behavior toward her. No doubt she wasn't a fan of love 'em and leave 'em types. Very illuminating.

He picked up a royal blue-and-gold pom-pom that had

been sticking out of a tall plastic cup on her desk, giving it a couple of shakes. *Go team.* He'd heard about American cheerleaders. He wondered if maybe Gisele had been one, and tried to picture her in that short skirt, doing those fancy moves. Did her skirt flit up, revealing thin white trunks and making you guess whether she wore underwear beneath them? The idea of stripping her out of her cheerleader uniform made his cock swell beneath his towel. Hell, he could think about Gisele whipping up blueberry pancakes at this point and it would give him a hard-on he'd need to take care of. This vow of chastity was messing with both of his heads, big-time.

"What the hell do you think you're doing in my room?"

Tomasso jumped at the sound and turned to see Gisele standing in the doorway, her face a sort of apoplectic red that didn't come naturally, except maybe in overripe tomatoes. Well, if he thought he'd angered her already, he had the distinct impression he was about to learn that hell hath no fury like a woman who's being snooped on.

Chapter Thirteen

GISELE had never given birth before and truly could not imagine what that experience was like. But right now, at this very moment in time, she felt as if she could easily birth a cow, maybe even a six-ton elephant. Her fury was so great she felt the need to expel some mountainous something from her loins. How dare he nose about her room as if he was entitled to? Conversely, how dare he look so damned sexy in just a towel—a towel beneath which he couldn't even conceal the swell of his cock? And would the axiom of that be how the hell could Gisele be filled with rage and yet so turned on, all at the same time? In addition, what was it about sneaking around her bedroom that so obviously turned him on?

Part of her wanted to flail her fists against his (broad, sexy) chest, because she was angry he'd invaded her private space. But another part of her simply yearned to slide her fingers coyly beneath the towel that rested around his waist so suggestively, low-slung as it was from hip to beautiful hip. Just use one finger to pull, ever so gently, till it fluttered to the ground, allowing her to expose his (very large and hard) private bits as he'd exposed hers.

It had been a week of conflicting temptations for Gisele: the desire to exact revenge on him for dumping her so ingloriously somehow did a bizarre tango with her molar-clenching need to see if she could make him regret his earlier ill-conceived decision. Maybe combine it all into a slick-bodied, heavy-panting revenge fuck, even though that wasn't her style. The revenge part. She'd be all up for the sweating and heavy breathing… and certainly the fucking bit. It had been ages since she'd had sex, and she felt sure that even commitment-free sex with Tomasso would be hot as hell. Or *caldissimo*, as the Italians would say. She'd never had that experience before: going for broke just to get it out of her system, feelings be damned.

But never in her life had she had to tamp down such a tremulous craving for a man. Perhaps it was because she'd never dated anyone who challenged her. The closest she came to that was kid from her high school, Stevie Mincer, who, after going out with her for four months (and making it all the way to third base, natch), decided to run against her for student council president, which displeased Gisele immensely. That sort of challenge didn't exactly blow her skirt. But this thing between her and Tomasso—well, this sexual tension was simmering between them like a witch's brew, sending heated fingers of sensual suggestion coiling around her mind like some snake charmer whose tune lulls a cobra into doing things that go against its very instincts.

"Look, Gisele," he said, dropping the pom-pom in his haste. "I'm sorry for this." He spread out his hands, motioning to the span of her room.

She stood there, silently, arms crossed, letting him stew in his guilt for a minute.

"You see, I just got out of the shower"—he motioned to his towel, which barely obscured what was lurking beneath—"and realized my underwear was in the dryer. So

I came down the hall to get it and noticed your door was open and your lights on. I came in to see if you were in here, fully intending to shut off the lights and close the door—"

"But—"

"But somehow I got distracted." His face turned red. He seemed actually embarrassed, which she found somewhat charming.

"By?"

"By trying to figure out you." He shrugged. "All week long you've been nothing but hostile to me and I get that I must have upset you when things got complicated and I backed off, but my aim was pure. I was only trying to be up front and honest. My intention wasn't to hurt your feelings or make you feel bad about yourself. But then I showed up here and was the sole object of your wrath. I couldn't understand why you wanted to hate me so much. I guess maybe I thought I could find a clue to something about you in here."

Gisele leaned against her door, feeling a little defeated. It was hard work holding a grudge. She remembered one time reading this story about how warring factions who were dug into those horrible mud trenches in France during World War I surfaced from their hiding places during Christmas to play soccer and consort with their enemies. Sadly that truce only lasted for a few days, but it must have been such a relief from the constant agitation and stress of combat.

She thought it might be nice to declare her own version of détente, though for some reason she didn't know how to implement it.

"And what did you find out about me?" She lifted a

brow.

He paused, taking a deep sigh. "I learned you lost your mamma at a young age and that she was a kind woman who did lots of wonderful charitable deeds."

Gisele nodded. That would be an understatement. Her mother spent many hours each week volunteering with the most underserved people in society. She helped teach women in prison to read. She taught English as a Second Language to immigrants. She knitted blankets for orphaned babies. She helped poor people with rides to the hospital for chemotherapy and radiation treatments. Her mother was a powerhouse of a woman and had packed a lot of living into her short life.

"What else did you learn?"

"That your father must have taken up with a much younger woman." He tilted his head toward her. "I'm sorry, Gisele."

She shook her head. It was never something she wanted to talk about. Life was much easier when he was no longer a part of it. Remembering how he'd abandoned his family, how her mother sobbed herself to sleep each night, it was too painful for Gisele to resurrect.

"Anything else, while you were snooping around?"

"Looks like you lettered in varsity soccer one year." He smiled and picked up the pom-pom. "But I was more intrigued by this, trying to imagine you in a cute little cheerleader costume."

All that insight, and then in typical male fashion, it comes down some twisted sexual fantasy. Although perhaps twisted was the wrong word. More like imaginative. She closed her eyes and thought about if she was truly brave, how she could dig into the bowels of her closet and unearth that cheerleading uniform. Maybe she could chant a cheer or show him how limber she was by doing a split or two. Then she'd see a rise from that snake-charming bath towel of his.

Although maybe *she* was the real snake charmer. Maybe it was the idea of her that had aroused him so much. And his arousal had, in turn, dampened her panties. Make that, soaked them.

She extended her arm and motioned with her finger for him to turn around.

Tomasso looked at her, his eyes questioning. She simply nodded and twirled her finger again.

He reached his arms out to the side, then slowly turned around, giving Gisele a 360-degree view of Tomasso Romeo in almost all his glory.

She nodded once more, then stepped into the room, close enough to reach out her hand and pull the towel out where it had been tucked in, barely securing it to his waist. The towel dropped, revealing his ever-hardening cock.

"Put your hands on it." She pointed at him.

He knit his brows but followed her orders and wrapped both hands around his erection. He could barely disguise how good it must have felt, with relief washing over his face.

"I want to watch you," she said, settling herself on the bed, leaning against the pillows. She kicked her boots off and made herself comfortable as though preparing to watch the TV in front of her, while Tomasso stood before her, waiting for her instructions.

"Go on, I want you to make yourself come."

Chapter Fourteen

TOMASSO groaned. What an impertinent, sassy little minx Miss Gisele Hornsby was. Gisele Horny. He liked that name much better. In a million years he never would have expected such a directive from her lips. He felt relieved she didn't want him to stand against the wall while she aimed darts at his dick. No. She wanted him to masturbate while she watched: reward instead of punishment for his bad deeds. Well, what the lady wants…

He stood before her, feeling a bit like a male stripper, only with nothing to strip off. He was perfectly comfortable in his own body, though never before had he actually jacked off for an audience. But he was game for anything.

He licked his hand, then rubbed his palm on the tip of his cock to capture the moisture that had already gathered there. Wrapping his fist around himself, he tugged and pulled, twisting his wrist as his cock hardened even more beneath his fingers. Soon, his other hand reached down to play with his balls, and in no time, he felt them tighten as his arousal gained steam in his body, his desire to come coupled with his latent fantasy of having Gisele finish what she'd started back in Monaforte, with her warm, soft, wet lips sliding over his head, slipping down the hard length of him, sucking hard, pulling the come from deep within him.

Christ, he'd thought about that a hundred times since that night, and here she was, so close yet so far.

His hand moved faster and he opened his eyes to see Gisele transfixed on him, her eyes scanning the hard planes of his abdomen, the rapid play of his hands on his dick. He could feel the momentum overtaking him and his knees grew weak as he tensed, shouting out her name as he came in jerking streams across his stomach and fingers. It was hard to recall a time he felt more turned on than he did putting on that show for her, fully dressed, on her throne of pillows, purely a spectator but obviously enjoying every minute of it herself.

Gisele hadn't quite considered the follow-through on this one. What does one do after ordering a naked man to masturbate in front of you in your bedroom? Was there official protocol for this?

What she actually desired was to crook her finger and beckon him to come to her and work *his* magical fingers—the ones he'd so brilliantly used on himself—to bring her to climax as well. Because if her panties were damp before, they were soaking now, after she'd watched with bated breath as he brought himself to orgasm.

He stood there, his eyes fixed on hers, almost defying her to make the next move. But she froze, unable to stand down from her own obstinate position. Finally, he yielded.

"I think I might need to clean up a bit, so, if you'll

excuse me." He backed out of the room, bending over to grab his towel as he left.

Well, that wasn't exactly what she'd planned for when she'd come home late. Here she thought she'd throw together a quick dinner and go to sleep. Instead, she was going to simmer just below the boiling point for the rest of the night.

Chapter Fifteen

TOMASSO had been prepping his wood for the past several days to get started on his figurehead. He'd laminated planks of island beech, glued them together in stages, making sure the wood grain fell correctly in areas of detailed carving such as the head and hands. Once the pieces were laminated into a large block, he used a chainsaw to remove large pieces to get the wood into workable condition. Embedded into the body of the figurehead were steel plates—between the shoulder blades and behind the knees—so he had to take care not to strike that with his saw.

Once he had the general shape, he began using smaller tools to finesse the wood into the shapes he wanted. It was essential to make sure the proportions were correct and that bones and muscles would appear the way they would on a real person. For the initial carve, he would leave everything larger scale since he could always carve away the excess to achieve the final proportions.

He was excited about this project and knew in his gut it would be his best yet. Which meant that each day, he arrived earlier to allow himself more time to dedicate to it, and each night he left even later. The upside was that it took his mind off Gisele. At this point, he hardly trusted himself alone with her in the house after what had transpired last week. He'd like nothing more than to turn the tables on her, but unless things radically changed, he'd never have the opportunity. He was nothing if not resourceful, though. He'd find a way to pierce her armor. It just might take awhile.

He'd spent his entire Saturday at the warehouse and was famished. He stopped at a store on the way back to grab ingredients for dinner, picked up a bottle of wine, and planned to kick back with a book for the evening. He'd brought in firewood earlier in the week. With any luck, Gisele would be out and he could make a fire in the living room and relax with no hassles for being in her breathing space.

He climbed the steps of the brownstone and kicked off excess snow from his hiking boots before entering the house. It was silent, but for the whir of the furnace. He took that as an all-clear sign that he could cross the demilitarized zone and use the entire kitchen.

Once in the kitchen, he began prepping his meal, chopping basil and parsley, sautéing garlic and shallots in olive oil, searing sausage in another pan. He put the water on to boil for the fresh pasta he'd purchased, then added some shrimp to the garlic mixture, shaking the hot pan repeatedly until they turned pink under his ministrations. He threw in some chopped tomatoes, a splash of clam juice, then put the pasta on to boil while the sauce cooked down for a few minutes. He took advantage of the lag time to open a bottle of Chianti Riserva before tossing in the basil and parsley. As the pasta drained, he added a few tablespoons of starchy pasta water to the sauce to thicken it up a bit, then mixed the pasta with it all.

He was so busy, with his back to the doorway, that he didn't even hear anyone entering the kitchen.

"Well, well, well," said a sultry woman's voice. "If it's not tall, dark, and packing."

He turned to see a lithe, statuesque woman with cascading dark hair that fell in waves over her shoulders. She had deep brown eyes, high cheekbones, and wore a bright slash of cherry red on her lips, which she licked sensuously.

"I'd heard you were a man of good taste, but I thought that meant you tasted particularly delicious." She laughed at her joke and took a few steps toward him, extending her hand. "Forgive the intrusion. I'm Sophie Pellegrino. I work with Gisele. We have plans for this evening, so I decided to swing by and pick her up to make things simpler. Little did I know I'd meet the international man of mystery! I'm so excited. And now I can report that Gisele grossly underestimated your sex appeal." She eyed him up and down as if she was about to take a bite. "And what have we here?" She reached for a spoon next to the pan and dipped it in, lifting it to her lips to taste. "Oh, God." Her eyes rolled back in her head, and she dipped the spoon in a second time. "I hope this isn't rude of me to double dip, but seriously, I need to taste this again."

Tomasso nodded at her. "You approve, then?"

"Oh, honey." She slapped her arm against his shoulder. "Not only do I approve, I might try to bring you home with me, so you can make this for me. Like every day."

Tomasso tipped the bowl he'd filled toward her. "Be my guest."

She put her hands up in the air. "But it's your dinner. I couldn't take that from you."

"No worries. There's plenty more where that came from. Go ahead. *Buon appetito.*" He poured her a glass of wine and motioned for her to sit down at the kitchen bar with him.

"And he speaks such perfect Italian," Sophie said as if speaking to an audience.

"I suppose we've not formally met," he said. "I'm Tomasso. Tomasso Romeo."

She grinned as she slipped a forkful of pasta past her bright red lips. "Romeo, oh Romeo, wherefore art thou?" She fluttered her eyelashes playfully. "I am going to have to ask Miss Gisele where she's been hiding you. And why."

Her text message dinged and she held up a finger to Tomasso.

"If you'll forgive me for one moment, I need to let Justin in."

Tomasso could hear a commotion at the front door and soon Sophie returned with a man.

"Justin, this is the hunk Gisele has been keeping from us. All the way from Italy—as in the land of handsome Italian men—mind you. Tomasso, meet Justin, my assistant."

He shook his head. "Assistant *producer*. There's a big difference." He sized up Tomasso and let out a whistle.

"Right?" Sophie said with a conspiratorial nod. "That Gisele needs to have her head examined."

Tomasso could only imagine what she was talking about, but he did presume Giselle would be less than happy when she found him befriending her work colleagues.

"I don't suppose there's any minuscule chance you bat for the home team?" Justin said, his eyes imploring.

"That's a baseball reference, Justin," Sophie said.

"They play soccer in Italy. I think you might need to say 'kick with the right foot' or something like that."

"That doesn't make any sense," he said. "Why don't I just come out and ask if he likes men."

"Based on what Gisele's told me, I'm pretty sure it's safe to say no."

Tomasso lifted his eyebrow, wondering how much Sophie knew about the two of them. Perhaps they would provide the perfect segue he needed to get under her skin more easily.

Justin rifled through a few drawers till he found a fork, and stuck it into the dwindling pile of pasta on Sophie's plate and took a bite. "Wow," he said, his mouth full. "This man can cook too. Let's find that girl and straighten her out."

"Find what girl?" All three heads turned to see Gisele enter the room. She had on a short black leather dress with a lace overlay and thigh-high black boots that about made Tomasso's legs turn to jelly. He immediately discarded his prior fantasy involving her sandals and decided he needed to see her with those boots and nothing else.

"Justin was just saying what an amazing cook and prime candidate for his team your Italian friend is," Sophie said, drumming her fingernails on the granite countertop.

Gisele rolled her eyes. "This is why I don't invite you over here. There's absolutely no reason to mix boarders with pleasure."

Sophie tsked her friend. "Now, now, Gisele." She wagged her finger, chastening her. "I for one am most grateful to finally meet this boy wonder. Make that man wonder. I think he's delightful. In fact, I vote we bring him along with us tonight. We could use a little excitement to spice up our otherwise dull social lives. In the interest of international relations, I say we invite Tomasso along for the ride. All in favor say aye." She gave her friend a wink.

"Aye," Sophie and Justin said in near unison.

Six sets of eyes settled on Gisele, whose lips were pursed shut.

"Aye." Gisele, Sophie, and Justin turned to see Tomasso, his hand raised in approval. "Thanks so much for the invitation. I'd love to join you."

Chapter Sixteen

"I cannot believe you betrayed me like this." Gisele was giving her friend a hard time as they stood at the far end of the bar trying to flag one of the bartenders for drinks.

"Betray you? I was only trying to facilitate things for you because you seem incapable of figuring out how to do it yourself. As if it's hard to figure out: insert tab A into slot B. And good God, I bet he's got one hell of a tab A."

"How many times do I have to tell you I'm not interested in him? Or his slot or tab or whatever." Gisele growled as she handed the bartender her credit card and grabbed the four bottles of beer after she signed the receipt.

"Okay, so are you good if I try my hand at your Romeo?"

"Please. He's not my Romeo." Gisele took a long swig of beer as they worked their way through the crowd to the table in the back where the guys were sitting.

"In that case, I'll consider him fair game." Sophie tipped her beer bottle to her friend's. "All's fair in love and war."

They returned to the table and Sophie settled into the seat nearest to Tomasso. She leaned her head close to his, and before long, the two were engrossed in conversation, beyond earshot over the throbbing sounds of electronica blaring in the background.

Soon Tomasso stood, grabbing Sophie's hand and leading her out toward the throng of people dancing to the pulsing beat.

Gisele glared at Sophie once they faced away from her.

"I saw that," Justin said.

"What?"

"That little green-eyed monster that just reared its ugly head."

"What? You think I'm jealous or something?" Gisele feigned a yawn. "That's preposterous."

"So then you're good if Sophie has her wicked way with the Italian Stallion?"

Gisele looked at him with a deadpan glare. She held up her thumb, enumerating her point. "First of all, I know Sophie, and she would never do that to me." She lifted her pointer finger. "Second, he's not mine anyhow."

Justin pointed a finger at her. "You said Sophie would never do that to you. But it isn't doing anything to you if he's not your man."

Gisele shook her head and swilled her beer. "Gah! Would everyone please stop trying to make this something it's not? We gave it a go and it didn't work out. End of story. No big deal."

They gazed out at the dance floor where Sophie and Tomasso seemed to be sinuously moving to the music as one, Sophie's ass pressed to Tomasso's crotch. What the hell?

"They look good together, don't they?" Justin said, a sly grin breaking across his face.

"Absolutely perfect. I couldn't have chosen a better couple."

"I was just thinking that myself."

"Fine. I hear you loud and clear. Enough!"

"Okay, then, but don't say I didn't warn you."

"You know, I think I'm ready to get out of here."

"Wait—we can't leave when they're still out there."

"I'm totally fine. Just stay put. I'm a big girl and I can handle myself, despite my brother's beliefs to the contrary." She stood and slipped into the crowd and disappeared out the door before Justin could even run after her.

She had a reason for not wanting to include that Rotten Romeo in her social life. Because now, nothing good was happening in her life—all because he'd invaded her space. Or had he found a tiny opening in the wall she'd built up? And was he invading her heart?

Chapter Seventeen

WHEN Tomasso returned the next morning, it would have been nearly time for brunch had Gisele kept to her usual brunch plans, but instead she'd stayed in. She heard the front door open and decided it was her prerogative to confront him.

"Look," she said as he entered the kitchen, a bag of groceries in his hand. "I don't think that was very considerate of you to disappear and not come home last night."

"Disappear?" he said. "Forgive me for my confusion, but wasn't it you who disappeared?"

She furrowed her brow. He had a point there. "I was tired and not having fun. You were busy coming on to Sophie and grinding against her on the dance floor and quite frankly, I'd had enough."

Tomasso laughed. "Coming on to Sophie? You mean because she was nice to me and I spoke to her?"

"Oh, I saw the way you looked at her. You practically drooled all over her plate when she was sitting here last night."

"I beg to differ with you, Gisele. If there was any drooling going on, it was when I saw you in those fuck-me boots. The minute I took a look at you in those things, all I could think about was how badly I wanted to bury my cock inside of you with those boot-clad legs wrapped around my hips."

Gisele's eyes opened wide. "Come again?"

"Exactly. I'd like nothing more than to come again, preferably at the same time as you while you're wearing those amazing boots." He looked down at her legs, currently clad in a pair of loose-fitting pajama bottoms with panda bears on them. "Though exotic Chinese animals would do in a pinch." He grinned at her.

"So you slept with her?" Gisele stared out the window at a cardinal picking a fight with a smaller bird near the bird feeder. She didn't want to hear it but she needed to get it out of the way.

"What do you think?"

"Of course you did. She's tall, thin, and beautiful. And you're a man."

Tomasso shrugged. "I don't kiss and tell."

"Neither do I."

"Oh, really? That's not the impression I got. It seems to me your friends know more about me than I do at this point. Including certain details that only you would have known."

"What are you talking about?" Gisele busied herself moving dishes from the dish drainer onto a towel for no apparent reason.

"Well, after several more drinks, Justin told me he'd heard that I had a, oh, how did he phrase it, an 'epic cock.'" Tomasso grinned. "It seems like he'd only have gleaned that kind of information from someone in the know."

Gisele looked down on the ground and dragged her toe across the floor. "Um…"

"I'm honored that you were so impressed with my God-given attributes. Although I'd be more honored if only you were interested in testing them out a bit. I'm sure I could impress you even further with my God-given moves."

She looked at him, so cocky and handsome and so darned right. It made her crazy that he knew she wanted him as much as he wanted her to want him. Maybe she could, just this one time, and finally get him out of her system, once and for all. He would be going back to Italy anyhow, and there could be no future in a relationship with him. Why not carpe that diem while the carpe'ing was good?

"I was just putting on a pot of chili," she said, changing the subject. "They're calling for a big snowstorm tonight. I thought it would be good to have something warm in case we get snowed in. Would you like to learn how to make some good old American chili?"

Tomasso nodded, no doubt happy she wasn't going to bury a cleaver in his back. Not that she'd ever do that. But still, the man made her so mad, and sometimes, she wasn't even sure what triggered it.

Yet now that she was warming up to the idea of warming up to Tomasso, how exactly would she go about doing so without it seeming awkward and forced?

Tomasso couldn't believe Gisele's change in demeanor last night. Was she that susceptible to a plain old bout of jealousy? And did she actually think her good friend would do that to her? The only reason he didn't come home last night was because Sophie persuaded him to stay out to make Gisele crazy. Sure he slept at Sophie's, but alone, in her guest bedroom. Sure Sophie was a beautiful woman, but she wasn't right for him. Besides, he wasn't about to risk losing his bet over anyone other than the woman he'd started things with in Monaforte. They had unfinished business to attend to.

They spent the afternoon cooking, of all things. Tomasso helped Gisele make her chili, and later, they decided to bake chocolate-chip cookies.

"So there's a great controversy surrounding this delicacy: to eat raw cookie dough and risk death by salmonella poisoning or to suffer the consequences of never knowing the joy of cookie dough," Gisele said as she stuffed a wad of it in her mouth. She scooped up a blob of dough onto her fingers and offered it to Tomasso, who tentatively nipped at it at first, but then slowly and sensuously licked it from her fingers. After most of the dough was gone, he pulled her index finger into his mouth and sucked on it, savoring the last delectable taste.

"I like these American baking traditions." He scooped some more dough onto his finger and swiped it onto her nose.

She tried to reach her tongue up to lick it off, to no avail. "Here, let me help you." Tomasso leaned down and dragged his tongue across the tip of her nose, deftly cleaning up the dough. He wanted nothing more than to continue where he'd started, but he could feel Gisele tense, so he backed off. He was going to have to take this very slowly. Like three-toed tree sloth slowly. At this rate, he'd get back in her pants by the time they were fifty.

Gisele turned to the cookie sheets in front of her. "We need to get these in the oven before, well, we just need to get these in the oven."

But taking it slowly was going to kill him, at this rate.

Chapter Eighteen

THEY spent much of the afternoon binge-watching TV shows in front of a roaring fire as a heavy snowfall descended. Eventually Gisele announced it would be fun to get out and experience the snow firsthand.

"Let's walk over to Central Park," she said. "It's only a few blocks away. It'll be good exercise after sitting around all afternoon."

She lent Tomasso some ski gloves and snow pants from her brother's clothing stockpile and stuffed some essential supplies in her pocket.

The snow was already hard to navigate and was up to midcalf along the sidewalks, with much more in the forecast. They were veritable trailblazers in this stuff. Once at the park, she put Tomasso to work.

"Time to test your snowman skills," she said. "You start working on the base and I'll get rolling the middle."

Little did Gisele know Tomasso had skills creating larger-than-life figures.

The two rolled snow into ever-larger balls and finally stacked them; then Gisele rolled a snowman head. She reached into her pocket and stuck a carrot into his face for a nose and made a mouth from a trail of paper clips. "It was all I could think of spur of the moment," she said. His eyes were two mismatched buttons she'd gathered from that random kitchen drawer that had always been the repository for things you didn't know what to do with. They found some sticks that would have to be good enough for his arms.

"So what're we going to call our creation?" she asked. "I think Frankenstein's already taken." Perhaps Frankenstein is what she should call the sexual tension that had been coiling between them, sending off sparks in every direction. It had become an out-of-control monster.

"How about Bianca? Though in that case, he is now a she."

"Bianca?"

"It means white in Italian. And Bianca is feminine."

"Bianca… I like it. Bianca it is."

"And Bianca, it seems, has some balls," Tomasso said as he scooped up a chunk of snow, rolled it into a tight circle, and threw it at Gisele's back.

"How dare you!" she said but leaned over and made an even larger snowball, lobbing it for a direct hit on his head.

He retaliated with a giant armful of snow, which he dumped all over her head. As he ran from her, she reached out a leg and tripped him. He landed face-first onto the soft snowpack, and she stumbled on top of him, her legs straddling him. He turned over and looked up at her, melted snow dripping down her face, her thick lashes sparkling with fresh flakes, making her bright blue eyes appear even larger. They stared at each other for a beat, both catching their breath. Gisele, her hands pressed to Tomasso's chest, stared back at him, then shook the snow off her head and body, all over his face.

She stood. "Come on, we best get back before it turns

dark."

Tomasso stared after her before standing up. It took him a minute to adjust himself, what with the unexpected presence, even in this frigid weather, of a very warm Gisele pressed to his very lonely cock. But once he got it calmed down, he chased her the rest of the way home.

It was dark by the time they returned, and after warming up in front of the fireplace, they dined on chili and cornbread and finished off the last of the IPAs in the fridge.

Soon Gisele was yawning, not so much due to tiredness, but because she wasn't sure where things were going and didn't know how to handle it. She decided the best plan of action would be to run away from whatever might happen if she let it. She was nothing if not a world-class coward, it seemed.

"Thanks for a surprisingly fun day," she said as she stood up to go to bed. "I'd better get some shut-eye because tomorrow's a workday."

Tomasso nodded outside the window, where snow was still blanketing the ground. "I'd be surprised if they expected you to work in this."

"It's New York," she said. "Barring unforeseen natural disasters, it's business as usual."

"In that case, I guess you'd best get your beauty sleep." He swatted her behind, which made her jump. "Sweet dreams, Gisele."

What in the hell was she doing? She kept going through things in her head again and again. Did she want to try to rekindle something between them? Or was that simply a fool's errand? It made far more sense to protect her heart, which had had enough damage inflicted on it in her young life. But then again, she wasn't a quitter—it made all the sense in the world to finish what she'd started. Or what he'd started. Or what they both seemed to need, like it or not.

She finished washing her face and brushing her teeth and ran a brush through her hair, then settled in beneath her comforter. Temperatures were supposed to get near zero tonight. Her goal was to stay warm, one way or another.

Nighttime is such a silent time. Only that quietude becomes deafening when the power goes out. Gisele woke to the noise of no noise at about half past two. Crap. No power meant no heat, which meant she was soon going to die of frostbite. Which could be a little melodramatic, but nevertheless, she hated shivering beneath blankets needlessly. A half hour after the power had stopped, she could feel the chill seeping beneath her comforter, even as she enveloped herself in the duvet for self-preservation's sake.

Ten minutes later, she had an even better idea of self-preservation: Parker's room had a fireplace in it. She knew that Tomasso had been taking advantage of that opportunity almost nightly. Things would still be toasty and warm in there.

She rose from the bed, draping her blanket around her like some sort of royal coronation robe, and grabbed her iPhone, turning on the flashlight on it so she could see as she walked down the darkened hallway, hoping for no chance encounters with strangers. She immediately thanked her brother for deciding she needed a companion in this raspy old house; she would have been terrified all alone in the place with no power, left to her vivid imagination when hearing the creaks and groans of a hundred-year-old townhouse in the pitch black. When she got to Tomasso's door, she couldn't decide whether to knock or perhaps slip in unnoticed. Maybe he wouldn't even realize she was there. She could settle down on the carpet near the fireplace and he'd be none the wiser.

After a few minutes of mental debate, she decided to quietly slip in and hope for the best. As she turned the doorknob, the screech was loud enough to wake the dead. So much for dodging the man's radar.

"Gisele? Is that you?"

"Sorry to wake you, but my room is freezing cold. We lost power and I knew you'd have the fireplace going in here."

She glanced over at it and noticed there were still some

embers smoldering, but it was hardly going to do the job as is.

"Here, let me help you." He climbed out of bed, tossed a few fire-starter sticks onto the embers, piled some wood on top, and using the bellows, forced air onto the pile to encourage the wood to catch fire. Within minutes the fireplace glowed orange with flames licking toward the flue.

"Now, let's get you back into bed."

"If you don't mind, I'm fine right here in front of the fire. I have a blanket, I'm easy."

"What sort of gentleman would I be if I allowed you to sleep on the floor? If anything, I'll take this spot, and you can sleep in the bed."

Gisele waved him away. "Absolutely not!"

"Well in that case"—Tomasso pointed at the bed—"it's a big enough bed that you can take one side and I'll take the other. And never the twain shall meet." He gave her a reassuring wink.

Gisele hesitated. Somewhere in her mind, she had almost been prepared to beg for this very scenario, but now that it was presented to her, she felt a bit shy about it.

Tomasso placed his arms over her shoulders and guided her to the far side of the bed. "I promise, I won't bite." A cloaked reference she, of course, remembered saying to him that first night in her palace apartment. Which seemed so very long ago. He tucked her in, even draped her blanket on top of his for added warmth. He returned to his side of the bed and climbed in. "I'm here if you need me."

She needed him, all right. More than she cared to admit. If only she knew how to let go and carpe that diem like she'd promised herself.

Chapter Nineteen

GISELE awoke with a loud shout not long after they had fallen asleep. Tomasso rolled over in bed toward her, immediately wrapping his arms around her to calm her.

"What is it?" he said.

Gisele shook her head. "Nothing. It was only a bad dream. I'm sorry to bother you again. Please, go back to sleep."

He pressed her head to his shoulder and whispered soothingly that everything would be okay. "You want to talk about it?"

She breathed heavily. Clearly the dream had unnerved her.

She sighed. "It's a recurring dream I have every few months. I'm at my mother's gravesite and my father and his new family show up and they just laugh at her. I get so angry but there's nothing I can do about it and I start banging my arms and swinging them at him. That's when I wake up."

"Man, he must have done quite a number on you."

"Let's just say that when your father abandons you, yeah, it messes with your head."

"And then you lose your mamma—"

"And a girl starts to realize it's better not to rely on

anyone else. Because sooner or later they leave."

"Does that count for big brothers as well?"

She nodded, pressing her face to his shoulder. He could smell the clean coconut scent of her hair as he softly kissed the top of her head.

"I'm guessing I did you no favors when I abruptly pulled back the way I did."

"Get in line." She heaved a sigh. "I'm used to it."

"I'm sorry, sweet girl." He crooned into her ear as he stroked her hair gently. "I didn't mean to hurt you any further. I hope you understand that wasn't my intention."

"Why did you do it, then?"

It was his turn to heave a sigh. "I had a girlfriend awhile ago. Her name was Liliana. She made my life exhaustingly hard. I tried to break it off and she started to stalk me. She spread rumors about me—even posted on my Facebook wall that I had a dick the size of an inchworm."

Gisele laughed. "Clearly she was misinformed."

He smiled against her head. "I guess she thought she'd hit me where it hurts. After all, what guy likes to have his manhood publicly questioned? It took a long time to finally get her to leave me alone. By then I'd spent money on lawyers, I had to change my cell phone number and e-mail addresses, I had to practically go into the witness protection program to hide from her. So I made a vow of celibacy. At least for a while."

"Was that before or after Luca's wedding?"

He shook his head. "Before, believe it or not. You see, I hadn't counted on meeting someone like you there. It rattled me to the core. We had such chemistry that very first night and we'd had so much fun. But then on top of it, I was planning to move to New York within a few weeks. It made no sense to start anything with anyone. Obviously I had no way of knowing this whole living arrangement was going to happen. I figured we were two ships passing in the night. And then I'd made a bet with my brother."

"A bet?"

"With Lorenzo. He was so certain I couldn't go without sex, we bet a thousand dollars that I could."

"But what about what happened between us in Monaforte?"

He shrugged. "Might have been splitting hairs, but I decided that wasn't officially sex, right? We didn't have intercourse. It was all foreplay. In my eyes, that didn't count."

She swatted at him. "It didn't count?"

"Not like that," he said. "I mean it didn't count toward the bet. But it did count as some of the best nonsex in my life. Although you did sort of leave me hanging."

"Sorry about that."

"Forgiven. But it was a moot point because then I resolved to be the responsible person I was trying to be and not lead you on or me on or anyone on."

"Hence you slinking away from me."

"I'd rather not view it as slinking away, but more like doing the right thing."

Tomasso put his finger to Gisele's chin, lifting it toward his face, and settled his lips over hers, placing soft, gentle kisses on them. "I love the quiet right now. When all we can hear is the sound of each other breathing." He pressed his tongue to her lips, encouraging her to open to him. Slowly she joined him, stroking her tongue along his, exploring his mouth.

"So is this doing the right thing now?" she said, her

breath coming faster. She pulled him close enough for his hardness to press against the sweet spot between her legs. "After all, I'd hate to be a bad influence on you."

"You could never be a bad influence on me," he said as he moved his fingers through her hair, massaging her scalp till she moaned.

"You could do that all night and you'd have me at your mercy, you know."

"You mean all this time you were shunning me and all I had to do was give you a simple scalp massage?" He rolled on top of her, his knees parting hers as he planted kisses around her face and along her neck. He lifted the hem of her T-shirt and raised it over her head, letting his eyes adjust to the dark enough to take a good long look at those beautiful breasts he had been craving for so long.

He returned his mouth to her neck and licked a hot trail along her cleavage, then to the underside of one breast, working his way up toward the luscious pink nipple, which he wrapped his lips around as he flicked it with his tongue. Gisele moaned as his left hand tweaked her other nipple, and she ground her hips against that now famous—at least amongst her friends—bulge he was packing in those boxer briefs.

Tomasso could not believe she'd finally opened herself to him. He took it slow, not risking a false move that would make her snap shut like an oyster. His hands searched her body, skirting her soft skin, his fingertips gently tracing circles around her nipples. Slowly his hands worked their way down her body. When he reached the waistband of her panda pajamas, he easily slid his fingers beneath the elastic, his wrists easing the hem down over her hips as his fingers sought the warmth of her slick center. When the pajamas were below the bottom edge of her ass, he tugged them the rest of the way off, urging her legs farther apart as his hands traced a sensual path between one leg and another, deliberately not touching the one spot where he knew she wanted him.

Gisele pressed her hips toward his hands, urging him onward.

"Oh, so you think you can tell me what to do?" he said, his mouth softly pressed to hers as he smiled.

She nodded, reaching for his hand and placing it right there, where they both wanted it to be. Tomasso slowly stroked through her wetness, his finger trailing a circle around her clit as she let out a moan. It was his turn to groan; he wanted so badly to slide his hard cock through her slick juices, finally pressing himself inside her warm center at last.

As if reading his mind, Gisele dragged down his boxer briefs and deftly used her foot to shove them the rest of the way down and off of him. She rolled him to the side and reached for his cock, so hard and desperate for her.

"I think I owe it to you to finish what I started," she said, shimmying down his body till she was finally where she'd left off all those weeks ago. She dragged her tongue around his swollen head, licking the pre-cum that had gathered at the tip. Her tongue continued to work on his cock till she finally took him into her warm mouth.

Tomasso thought he'd died and gone to heaven, feeling the pull and suck as she worked his cock, her hands gently squeezing his balls. But he knew he couldn't last; it had been too long and he'd been craving this moment for weeks. He reached beneath her arms and pulled her up. They were chest to chest, her nipples pressed to his, his

Blue Collar Romeo

cock impossibly near his desired target.

Gisele took the hint, rising to her knees, and straddled his body. She rubbed his cock along her lips, circling her clit, moaning as she did it, while Tomasso played with her nipples. The sight of her so engrossed in pleasure about did him in, and he reached for his cock, guiding it finally to her opening. Gisele slowly slid down over him, then waited a few beats. Tomasso thought he would die from the feeling of her hot pussy enveloping his dick. He needed to feel more and pressed his hips to her, motioning for her to do the same. She happily obliged, alternating grinding her hips in a circular motion with riding him like a wild mustang. Tomasso could feel his balls tightening, sparks shooting off beneath his eyelids, when Gisele's body trembled, the hot clutch of her pussy clamping hard on his cock. He couldn't hold off anymore, and he held her tight to him as he released deep within her body.

Chapter Twenty

"IT'S about forty degrees in here," Gisele said, wiping the sweat from her brow. "So why am I so hot?"

"What can I say?" Tomasso said. "I seem to have that effect on women."

"I'll say," she said. "So much so that I didn't even stick to my hard and fast rule of using a condom."

"I'm sorry," he said. "It all happened so fast. I should have made certain of that."

"Me too," she said. "But I didn't want to spoil the moment. Or give me a chance to chicken out again." She ran her fingers through his hair. "Besides, according to you, you've been celibate for ages, right? And I've not been with a guy in about a century. Plus, I'm on the pill. Except…"

"Except what?"

"You didn't really do anything with Sophie the other night, did you?"

Tomasso laughed. "Your friend Sophie is a wise, wise woman." He leaned forward and kissed her softly on the lips. "She assured me that you'd be burning with envy if you thought I was interested in her."

"Why, that dirty rat!" Gisele chuckled. "How dare she?" Only she wasn't all that mad because she was trailing her finger along the contours of his chest, pinching a nipple, then following that trail of hair on his belly as it worked its way toward her intended goal.

"I think she knows you better than you think she does," he said. "She said you were, oh, how did she phrase it? A weenie. She said you were a complete weenie and you'd rather miss out on the best sex in your life than take a chance when you feared there might be a risk."

Gisele knit her brows. "Curse that woman. She was right, of course."

"So do I have Sophie to thank for this sudden change of heart, or do I have Mother Nature?"

"Mother Nature?"

Tomasso pulled the comforter up over the two of them. Gisele, tucked into the crook of his arm, continued to dance her fingers across the hard contours of his body.

"Well, the snowstorm, the power going out. You coming in here to take advantage of the warmth of the fireplace."

Gisele felt she had to be truthful with him. "Now it's time for my confession," she said, her hand softly stroking the length of his soft cock, trying to coax it to come out to play some more. "I actually came in here to take advantage of you. The power being out sort of gave me permission to stop being, well, a weenie."

Tomasso rolled over on top of Gisele and captured her mouth with his. "I'm glad you finally came to your senses," he said as he kissed her mouth, her nose, her cheeks, and moved along her chin, till his tongue dragged along her ears, down her throat. "It seemed such a waste for us to be alone in this big old house, never able to take advantage of each other."

"So now that we're in the advantage-taking stage of

this relationship, what say we take advantage of that while we can?" Gisele wrapped her legs around his hips and locked her feet so that his hard length was nestled right between her legs. Tomasso reached his hands down and palmed the globes of her soft ass, kneading her flesh, pressing her body toward his hardness.

"Far it be it from me to not obey your every wish, your majesty," Tomasso said. "But I have one request."

Gisele arched her eyebrow. "And what might that be."

"Would you mind terribly putting on those thigh-high leather boots before we go any further?"

It didn't take long for Gisele to marvel at how much more enjoyable life was with Tomasso both under her roof and under her body. Whereas before, the two of them took pains to never be together in the same place, now each of them hurried home from work to take advantage of the short time they would have in each other's company before Tomasso had to return to Italy. Gisele didn't even want to think about what that would entail.

Tomasso had promised he'd soon bring her out to the warehouse to finally check out the project he'd been working on with such intent. Meanwhile, she wished he didn't have to go all the way to Brooklyn to work each day. Which gave her an idea. She waited for the first sunny day they'd had in weeks.

"I have something I'd like to show you," she said, a

twinkle in her eye.

"Does it involve us being naked?" He grinned at her.

She pondered that for a minute. "I hadn't thought about it but I suppose it could. Depending on how creative you actually are."

"Now I'm particularly intrigued."

"Then come on." She grabbed his hand and led him down another hallway, one he hadn't been down before, because, well, he'd been warned to stay away from just about everything in the house. They came to a doorway that opened to a small elevator. "Hop in," she said, patting his butt to encourage him in.

"Aren't you full of surprises?" He leaned forward and kissed her.

She latched the door shut and pressed the button to the top floor, and the somewhat rickety contraption slowly rose until it came to a stop. She unlatched the door and opened it, leading him into a spacious, bright, open room, filled with windows and sunlight.

"An artist's studio," she said, spreading her arms out to show him.

"Indeed," he said. "I fantasized about something like this in a New York City brownstone. I can hardly believe you've had this here all along. And it's unused!"

"And here I thought you'd fantasized about me, not about a room." She pushed her lip out in a fake pout. "But you have a point—it is unused. So perhaps we could at least christen it."

She loved that it only took two people and the boundless sexual desire coursing through them to find plenty of entertainment in an empty room.

"I love that your dirty mind is in tune with mine," he

said, lifting her up and wrapping her legs around his. "Because I can't think of a better use for this space than what I have planned for it right now."

His hands had already started shifting her sweatshirt off her. "I can't tell you how it pleases me that you didn't even bother to put a bra on. It's as if you wanted to be at the ready for me."

"Well, duh," she said, pulling his T-shirt over his head, running her hands over his chest. "But what to do about these troubling jeans?"

Tomasso set her down briefly, quickly toed off his shoes, pulled down his jeans, and stripped Gisele's yoga pants off her body.

"Now get back here," he said, lifting her up again, pressing her against the wall as he slid his cock inside her.

"Your wish is my command." She groaned into his mouth as his cock filled her to the hilt. "After all, we do need to christen your very first artist's studio."

"You mean I can actually use this?"

She nodded. "As long as you keep doing this to me, you can use it, you can use me. Whatever you want, just fuck me."

"My six favorite words in the English language."

Chapter Twenty-one

FINALLY the day had arrived. Tomasso was nervous about revealing the focus of his many intensive hours of work to Gisele. He worried she wouldn't embrace it as he had. But at last, he was learning to trust, both in her and in his gut, and he had to simply go with it. He held her hand tightly as they stepped off the bus and walked the five blocks to the warehouse. It was one of those days that held the promise of spring looming in the not too distant future: the sun was out and warm enough to have started melting the piles of blackened slush that are the hallmark of late winter in the Northeast.

"A few more blocks and we might even break a sweat," he said, smiling. He didn't say it was more like a flop sweat that threatened to overtake him at any minute. It was a Sunday; he chose a weekend day for the big reveal so that they could be alone. He didn't want Grady to witness his humiliation if Gisele hated it and stormed out.

He fumbled with the door lock, nervousness seeming to overtake him every which way. Eventually he unlocked the door and they entered the massive space.

"Holy cow," Gisele said, spinning around in wonderment, first at the sheer size of the workshop, then at the many projects she noticed lined up throughout the vast hall.

She dragged her hand along a wooden statue of a man sitting in a chair, a small dog nestled in his lap. "This is amazing."

"It's a special project Grady's been working on for a dear friend whose dog passed away recently."

"Wow. Some friend. It's beautiful." She stared into the statue's eyes. "And so lifelike, but it's made of wood."

"An artisan with the right ability can make even something as inanimate as a piece of wood come to life. Pretty amazing, isn't it?"

"Magnificent. I can see why this excites you."

He squeezed her hand. "Mind you, not nearly as much as you excite me."

She kissed him. "I can't wait to see what you've been making."

They held hands as he led her through the workshop, pointing out the many projects that had occupied an untold number of hours over the past few months. "This scroll will be part of a fireplace in a home in Manhattan." He pointed to a piece propped up on a workbench.

"Such beautiful detail. I'm so impressed! I mean, I knew you were into this stuff, but Tomasso, you're really good!"

He shrugged. As much as he loved doing this, he felt a little weird being the object of accolades for it. It's what he loved to do.

"Maybe you want to hold off on your assessment until you see the pièce de résistance." His mouth turned up in a grin on one side. He was nervous as they strolled along a lengthy corridor of the warehouse and he pointed out a beautiful mahogany fireplace surround, some wood plinths, and other architectural flourishes all awaiting their final destination where they would grace someone's home.

At the far end of the cavernous space, they came to a large project draped completely in white canvas.

Tomasso winced. "Okay, so here's the deal. If you don't like it, it's okay to tell me so. You won't hurt my feelings. Obviously beauty is in the eye of the beholder and all that."

"Of course I'll love it. Whatever it is, it's a creation of your mind and your hands."

"You might want to wait until you see it to make that final determination."

"I'm deathly curious now."

"I know I told you I have a fascination with maritime woodwork. Particularly figureheads, which have long held a place in history for those whose lives were inextricably tied to the sea. Figureheads carry with them great lore and often were imbued, at least in the captain's and sailors' minds, with special powers to keep their ship safe from the many dangers that were inherent in sailing stormy seas. Figureheads to me personify the romance of the seas. And I've long dreamed of creating my very own figurehead, even though I don't have a ship to attach it to. Nor do I have any idea where I would put this thing. But I felt the need to make it. The only thing was, what to make? Throughout history, many different figures graced the prows of sailing vessels: mythical characters, Viking gods, crests of powerful nations, even fearsome creatures to ward bad spirits off. But in my mind's eye, the quintessential figurehead is that of a mermaid—a beautiful half woman, half fish, with her provocative figure and mesmerizing charms. I knew it was what I wanted to make. But what mermaid?"

Gisele playfully smacked his arm. "Enough with the talk, already, let's see it."

"But I rehearsed this and everything." He smiled at her as he reached for the corner of the tarp and pulled it to unveil his own little masterpiece.

Gisele stood back as he retracted the cloth, inch by inch until before her stood a larger-than-life mermaid. That looked remarkably like… her. She gasped. Right in front of her stood the most lifelike rendering of herself imaginable, from her long, wavy hair that draped over her strong shoulders, to the bright blue eyes that Tomasso always told her he loved. The mermaid clutched one bare breast sensuously while her other hand pressed against a decorative wooden perch upon which her lower fishtail half—with scales of turquoise, her favorite color—rested suggestively as if she were riding the thing for her own pleasure. This mermaid looked to be in a near state of ecstasy. Of her own doing.

Gisele's eyes opened wide. "Oh, my God. Tomasso. I'm speechless."

He stood frozen in place for a moment, staring at her. "So?"

She practically jumped him, wrapping her legs around him as she pulled him to her and gave him a long, slow kiss.

When they finally came up for air, he looked into her eyes. "Does this mean you like it?"

"Tomasso, it's the most incredible thing I've ever seen. But, I mean, why me?"

"That night, when you found me in your room. And you made me touch myself for your pleasure. I'd been struggling to come up with the perfect figurehead to carve. There were so many options. But at that moment, I realized you were my figurehead, Gisele. You, with that blond hair that makes me think of the very first time we were together every time I look at it. And those intriguing eyes, looking up at me that night while you focused your attention on pleasuring me as you did. No issues, no reservations, just there to enjoy yourself and me. And then when you caught me in your room, and you made me do that, and it was such a damned turn-on. I'd wanted so badly to flip the tables and make you return the favor, but I knew I couldn't. You were so skittish, there was no way that was going to happen. That's why I decided you would be my mermaid, and my figurehead could do whatever I wanted her to do. Which is what you see before you. I was sorely tempted to have her wearing those fuck-me boots of yours, but couldn't figure out how to do that since she doesn't have legs."

She laughed. "Just as well. But truly, Tomasso, this is unbelievable. And you kept this from me this whole time."

"Well, as much as I'd have loved it, it's not like I could up and move a ten-foot wooden statue to the artist's loft in your place. That made it much easier to keep it from you. Besides, I was worried you'd hate it."

Her eyes grew wide. "Why would I ever hate something so beautiful, crafted with your masterful hands?"

"Well, your mermaid doppelganger is getting herself off on a wooden mount while toying with her breasts."

Gisele laughed. "I should be so lucky to have the

opportunity." She ran her fingers through her hair. "But it is giving me ideas." She shrugged off her coat and began pushing his down his arms. "You don't mind if we have an audience do you?"

They both turned to look at the mermaid, who seemed a bit preoccupied. "I'm pretty sure she'd approve," he said as he lifted Gisele's shirt. "Birds of a feather and all."

"Or mermaids."

"Let's give her something to talk about."

"It would be my pleasure, Captain."

He smiled. "And as long as we can please each other, I think things will be just fine."

"Then shut up and start pleasing."

"Your wish is my command."

Thank you so much for reading *Blue Collar Romeo*! I hope you enjoyed it! If so, please help others find this book:

1. Help other people find this book by writing a review.

2. Sign up for my new releases email so you can find out about the next book as soon as it's available and get fun giveaways.
http://eepurl.com/baaewn

3. Like my Facebook page.
www.facebook.com/jennygardinerbooks

And I love to hear from readers! Let me know what you think about my books! You can write to me at jenny@jennygardiner.net, and visit me on the web at www.jennygardiner.net.

Turn the page for a sneak peek of the next book in The Royal Romeos – **Silver Spoon Romeo**!

Silver Spoon Romeo

Chapter One

SOPHIE Pellegrino had grown weary of famous people who did idiotic things. Which didn't bode well for her professionally, considering she'd been producing a sort of soul-exposing (and not in a good way), mea culpa-type of reality show that featured celebrities who'd landed themselves in a pickle for all sorts of embarrassing reasons. Usually it was bad behavior induced by too much Cuervo, recreational drugs, arrogance, or a combination thereof, and sometimes it was out of sheer stupidity: just because you were a famous celebrity didn't mean you had a brain that served you well.

She'd produced stories about an actress found running naked down Rodeo Drive while shouting like a fishmonger that her actor-boyfriend was having sex with the Dalai Lama (she claimed a bad case of exhaustion). And the famous reality TV shrink who it turned out had three families in three different countries (he chalked it up to too many anxiety meds).

Then there was the married actor and father of three who got caught on camera in a compromising position with a child star on the set of his latest film (he was a big fan of Ecstasy, both the drug and the state of). Sophie just shook her head on that one, wondering what the hell was wrong with the man that he couldn't see that nothing good was going to come of that once he got busted. And they always got caught. Which boded well for her show: there was never a dearth of sordid stories with which to regale her audience. She sometimes wondered if celebrities did some of this stuff just to remain relevant, which would be sort of pathetic but not too surprising. Sometimes those who feasted at the banquet of fame starved to death without it, and were willing to settle for notoriety instead.

She was beginning to feel like she needed a long, hot soak after work each night, not so much to relax, but rather to cleanse the figurative muck off of her after dealing with so many unseemly people who thought fame was a license to behave not just badly but abhorrently.

So the timing could not have been better when her boss announced some big changes were looming.

"Soph, I've got some great news for you." Danny Slinger spoke like a human machine gun in a rapid-fire New York-accented banter as he slurped what was probably his eighth cup of high-octane coffee before noon. His mussed-up, salt-and-pepper hair hung over his eyes as if he couldn't be bothered to get it trimmed, and he was missing a button in his shirt. Among her best friends, Sophie tended to refer to Danny as a bit of a schlub, since he never seemed to put a scintilla of effort into personal maintenance. Nevertheless, she respected him professionally in spades. "You're getting your own show. Starting immediately—you're going to produce and host a lifestyles program featuring fantasy destinations."

Sophie squinted and cocked her head. "Is this a joke? Cause seriously, I don't think I can handle it if you tell me in five minutes you were just pulling my leg."

Danny took another swig of his coffee, his hyper-caffeinated brain causing the mug to tremble in his hands. "Would I lie to you?"

He mouth spread into one of those annoying grins you see when your poker opponent tells you he has four Jacks to beat your full house. The kind of smug look you'd usually want to wipe off a guy's face. Only for Danny it all worked.

"Uh, yeah," she said. "Remember that time you told me you'd landed that divorce-bound Brad Pitt interview and I was going to be in charge of it?"

He rolled his eyes and slapped the heel of his hand to his forehead. "Are you that dense?" He fixed his gaze on her. "It was April Fool's Day. You should've known that was a lie. Besides, don't you think I'd have taken on someone of his magnitude if we'd actually gotten him?"

"My first clue should have been that Brangelina—minus the 'ngelina'—would never do an interview for one of your tawdry shows."

He clutched his hands to his heart. "You're killing me, Pellegrino." He half pushed her away and fake-staggered a few steps. "Here I do you a solid and what do I get but disrespect?"

Sophie lifted her eyebrows in hope. "Wait. So you're telling me you're actually serious?"

"As a heart attack. Which you're going to give me if you turn this down."

"Are you kidding? I was beginning to think we needed to install a disinfectant room so that we could all cleanse ourselves after the show, the program's gotten so icky. I would love nothing more than to get away from *Gotcha* with my soul intact."

"Trust me when I say we could never have become so

Silver Spoon Romeo

icky without you. Consider this your reward for a job well done. You found the bottom of the barrel and you made it look like a Park Avenue penthouse. But I do recognize it's time to let my baby bird fly from the nest."

"You mean that shit-encrusted nest to which I'd have become glued if I stayed much longer?"

"One man's bird crap is another man's Emmy award-winning programming."

Sophie tipped her head in disbelief. "Daniel Slinger: you never earned an Emmy for that program."

"I'm just saying it's possible. Just because you think my show is catering to the lowest common denominator doesn't mean that those unwashed masses who inhale every episode and obsess about it on social media for days afterward don't think the show is a class act."

Sophie rolled her eyes. "More like a class action lawsuit waiting to happen." She waved her hands as if to erase the conversation. "But enough about that. I want to hear what you've got going for me. By the way, I feel the need to get it in writing that I no longer have to interview some pathetic attention-seeking D-level celebrity who's just been sprung from his fourth stint in rehab after going on a joyride with a monkey at the wheel while under the influence of a controlled substance."

Danny rubbed his hands together with glee. "That was one of our best shows this year!"

"Stop!" Sophie clasped at her head with her fingers.

"Okay, okay." He held his hands up in surrender. "So here's the deal. The men in suits want to take things in a new direction. They like your style and they want to give you free rein to show us what you can do. It's going to be an aspirational type of show—your viewers are going to want to be there in your shoes. Maybe even want to kill you to replace you in those shoes."

"So like a gladiator-style show? To the death and all that?"

Danny curled his lip in annoyance. "So little faith, my dear. It's like you don't think I have your best interest at heart." He petted her head. "Trust in the process, Grasshopper."

She shook her head. "Sorry. It's just hard to transition from sludge—I can't fathom a world of purity and joy."

"Well, then, prepare yourself. Because this is your baby to do with as you please. Think about what you would love to do—put your passion behind it. And then make a show out of it. Sky's the limit."

She looked skyward. "Seriously? Anything? Anywhere?"

"Within reason and within budget. Like we're not going to send you up in the Space Shuttle."

"Thank god."

"So give it some thought and get back to me. The executives are ready to move forward with this, so I'm giving you the weekend to decide. The important thing to know is that you're in charge: it's your baby, and you're the host. And don't fuck it up or my next show will be that gladiator-style one with me feeding you to the lions." He slurped some more coffee as he pointed toward the door. "Now go."

"Oh, my god," Gisele said as she took a sip of her wine. They'd gone to their favorite wine bar after work to discuss details of Sophie's new assignment. "This is like your dream. Like your dream of dreams. Like if someone asked you what your impossible-to-attain fantasy job would be, this would be it."

"I know. I keep pinching myself to be sure I'm not just sleeping."

"So what're you going to do?"

"With the sky being the limit, it's awfully hard to narrow it down to something more speicfic. I feel like I've been given a chance to eat the finest meal I've ever had but only get one stab at it—do I go for the sumptuous lobster thermidor or the potentially lethal Japanese pufferfish?"

Gisele held up her finger. "I think I can solve your problem. See, I was about to ask for some time off to go visit Tomasso." She'd recently fallen in love with Tomasso Romeo, a member of the Romeo family, which had run the world-famous Italian vineyard *Cantine dei Marchesi Romeo* for centuries. He'd been living in Manhattan under her roof while on a woodworking apprenticeship, but had recently returned home and she'd been pining for him badly. "Why don't you take the show to Chianti? Do a big thing with the Romeo family. Everyone knows Romeo wines, but does everyone know about the opulent lifestyle that comes with being a Romeo? Not to mention don't you think your audience—primarily women—would swoon madly for the Romeo men? One more handsome than the next?"

Justin Magruder, Sophie's long-time production assistant, piped in. "Now you're speaking my language. Hot Italian men. Sign me up."

The women laughed, and Sophie crossed her arms and rested her hand in her chin in thought. "Italy…" she said. "I could combine this with a search for my Italian roots. And my love of wine, and, well, my love of men, Italian or otherwise."

Justin fist-bumped her. "I'm with you, sister."

"Plus, I mean, all the biggest celebs hang there. George Clooney. Didn't Tom Cruise have one of his weddings there? Beyoncé, she's always on a damned yacht somewhere in Italy."

"You thinking what I'm thinking?" Gisele said, her blue eyes sparkling. She lifted her brow and tucked her long, wavy, blond hair behind her ears.

"Road trip to Tuscany?" Justin said as he flagged the waiter down and ordered a bottle of Prosecco.

When the waiter brought back the bottle and uncorked it with a pop, Justin stood up.

"This calls for a toast." He lifted his glass and held it to Sophie and Gisele's. "Here's to the best damned team *Gotcha* ever had and is now going to lose to the big leagues." He waved his fingers. "Sayonara *Gotcha*. And here's hoping we are drowning in the best wine and the best men Italy has to offer."

"Sorry, dude, I've already found my guy," Gisele said with a grin.

"Fine then maybe share some of that football team of a family with us. Sophie and I are looking for some Romeo

man-meat. Amiright, Soph?"

She laughed. "One thing at a time. I want to do this right, so job first, and with any luck the wine and men will follow."

Silver Spoon Romeo

coming June 13, 2017.

About the Author

Jenny Gardiner is the author of #1 Kindle Bestseller *Slim to None* and the award-winning novel *Sleeping with Ward Cleaver*. Her latest works are the *It's Reigning Men* series, featuring *Something in the Heir, Heir Today Gone Tomorrow, Bad to the Throne; Love is in the Heir, Shame of Thrones; Throne for a Loop; It's Getting Hot in Heir; A Court Gesture;* and her new Royal Romeos series, featuring *Red-Hot Romeo; Black Sheep Romeo, Red Carpet Romeo, Blue Collar Romeo,* and the upcoming *Silver Spoon Romeo*. She also published the memoir *Winging It: A Memoir of Caring for a Vengeful Parrot Who's Determined to Kill Me,* now re-titled *Bite Me: a Parrot, a Family and a Whole Lot of Flesh Wounds;* the novels *Anywhere but Here; Where the Heart Is;* the essay collection *Naked Man on Main Street,* and *Accidentally on Purpose* and *Compromising Positions* (writing as Erin Delany); and is a contributor to the humorous dog anthology *I'm Not the Biggest Bitch in This Relationship*.

Her work has been found in Ladies Home Journal, the Washington Post, Marie-Claire.com, and on NPR's Day to Day. She was also a columnist for Charlottesville's Daily Progress for over a decade, and is the Volunteer Coordinator for the Virginia Film Festival.

She has worked as a professional photographer, an orthodontic assistant (learning quite readily that she was not cut out for a career in polyester), a waitress (probably her highest-paying job), a TV reporter, a pre-obituary writer, as well as a publicist to a United States Senator (where she first learned to write fiction). She's photographed Prince Charles (and her assistant husband got him to chuckle!), Elizabeth Taylor, and the president of Uganda. She and her family and menagerie of pets now live a less exotic life in Virginia.

Visit Jenny at her website at www.jennygardiner.net where you can sign up for her newsletter, visit her blog, or find her on Facebook and Twitter. And every blue moon she'll post adorable pictures of her pets on Instagram as @thejennygardiner.